CONCRETE
JUNGLE

JACKSON
P R E S S

Copyright 2005 by Jackson Press Corp.
ISBN: 0-9769112-0-5

Art Direction/Design: Jason Claiborne / Sublime Visuals
Editors: Lene / Giselle Robinson

Library of Congress Congress Control Number 2005927112

First printing Jackson Press Corp. paperback June 2005

Printed In Canada

JacksonPress.net
P.O. Box 690344 Bronx, New York 10469

CONCRETE JUNGLE

Welcome to The Jungle

| Lene

Relax, while I take you on a trip to the jungle. No, it's not your average jungle where all the players have a role, but the concrete jungle of America. You see many can't recognize the jungle without Tarzan, Jane or Boy. Even though they are major participants they are not the only players. In the jungle there are no laws. The code is to eat or be eaten, devour or be devoured. A place where only the strong survive and the ignorant are in bliss.

Living in the jungle for many years has taught me many lessons. First of all is that the king is hard to spot. He doesn't wear a specific headdress, neither does he roar when he opens his mouth. He is a quiet king, a king who believes that he is superior to all of the other animals. He does not show his hand until the time is right. He is well respected, but he trusts no one, not even his own mother. It is the culture that he will never defy. He is the King and all other animals are inferior to him (so he believes). He is a strong fighter. And many are afraid of him, but he is not necessarily the smartest. He stalks his prey, attacks, and kills and then eats to his liken. He is unaware that while he is concentrated on his prey he too is being watched by someone.

The enemy of the Lion is the Hyena. The Hyena roams the streets at night and sleeps during the day. When he is awake it watches the lion as it kills its prey and then set out to take it away, laughing along the way. Just like the Lion the Hyena is a hunter, but it hides behind a mask so that it true identity is never known and it waits behind the scene until the time is right, and then it appears like a thief in the night. The hyena likes to run in a pack. The group mentality gives the Hyena confidence and insurance, he knows that there is power in numbers, and he lives and dies by that code.

The players, hustlers, dealers, and ladies of the evening are all major characters in the jungle, working almost 24 hours a day with very little soap and very little sleep. Eventually, they get to take a vacation in the esteem Rikers Island Hotel, but sooner or later their lease gets terminated and back into the jungle they go. Without a second thought they go back into the streets searching for old and new prey, because they know that everybody has a weakness. Love of money, searching for love, drugs, or just mere excitement pulls them into the darkest corners, where no sensible man dares to walk.

The jungle is a very different place at night. Lesbians, homosexuals, who hide in the closet during the day parade proudly down the streets of the village at night. They know that there is a trust, unity, code all of its own that no one dare to challenge, for if it is found out and the closet comes open, better is it to be dead, then deal with dishonor. Joy cometh in the morning when the closet is close and remains close until the secret compartment is opened again, every Skelton in its place.

Let us not forget the minute creatures that hide in the smallest nooks and crannies of the jungle. Up every tree, in every leaf, on every branch, even hiding in the owl's hole. Going about their daily chores without ever being seen by the human eye. They are the wife and husband abusers, child abusers, and cheaters. Who think that they go unnoticed as they walk across the picnic table in broad daylight. Unaware that the fly squatter is hidden waiting for the right moment then, SQUAT! Their dead, caught and their lives become so confused and they begin to wonder, where do I go from here?

You should not believe for one second that the jungle is full of murders, hustlers, and stick up kids. For yesterday these criminals were law abiding citizens, mothers and fathers from very functional families. What would make a blue collar worker turn into a murderer? And what would make a murderer turn into a snitch? What would make a snitch turn into an FBI informant? It's called SNAP! Yes, SNAP! Their minds have snapped. The everyday hustle and bustle of today's society is enough to make people steal from themselves, turn on their friends, and kill people that they love. With their fifteen minutes of fame, they become heroes, leaders, and causes for others to live. Just imagine it seeing your name written in the news paper, or even up in lights. Pleasure for fifteen minutes, running for the rest of your life.

The jungle has a beauty all of its own, its beauty does not go unnoticed. The smell of the first dew, the rising of the sun, the sweet sound of the birds singing, the quiet peace before the jungle awakes, a new day we've never seen, breathe taking.

Those who survive until the morning can tell you that it's not easy living in the jungle from day to day. The world is a stage and everyone is a player (William Shakespeare). You succeed according to how well you learn to play the game. Everyone must play whether they want to or not. All are key players even without knowing their roles. "It's a Dog Eat Dog World", and if your hungry enough the world is yours to attain. Survival is always linked to the physically and mentally fit; all others must wait for a miracle, or at least have one dollar and a dream.

The survivors of the game have a story to tell, but like most games there are only a few winners, and their names are well known. Playing the game whether you win or lose, could lose you self respect, dignity, and respect of others, what a high price to pay.

The players must remember that while living in the concrete jungle there are no set rules to follow, but playing in the game the rules are clearly set. Those who disagree or defy the rules will be punished either judged by twelve or carried by six.

The concrete jungle has billions of stories, some true and the others half truths, regardless of which one it is everyone has a story to tell.

With all its beauty and mystery, I can't think of any other place that I would want to be. For I was raised in the jungle, it's all that I know. For it is there that I can explore many different places, in my mind. I have traveled across the world. I have seen it all. There's no place I have not been, there's no place I wouldn't go. Every morning I open my window and I explore the world, one minute at a time.

Money Ova Everything

| A.J. Rivers

He had some nerve showing up here. Who even invited him? How dare he step his foot in this building? He is part of the reason why I am where I am today. If it wasn't for him, I'm sure I would have been better off. I'm willing to bet any amount of money that I wouldn't be right here right now. All of the crap he put me through. I still remember it like it was yesterday.

"So what are you sayin"? I screamed at Pee, unable to believe what I was hearing. I knew exactly what it was he was saying.

'All I'm sayin' is what's in it for me? I'm lookin' out for you. I'm giving you what you want and I ain't getting nuttin' in return. You can't always get suttin' for nuttin', Moe."

With that said, Pee turned his head to the left slightly and gazed beyond the deep tinted windows of the SC 400. He knew he was wrong and that's why he couldn't look me in the eye. So instead, here I was sitting, making eye contact with the brim of his baseball cap or rather, the side of his head.

"So, what about all the money I been spendin' wit you all summer?" I screamed. "I guess that's nuttin'. What my money ain't good enough for you? You fuckin' me on da prices already but dat ain't enough. Now you wanna fuck me for real, huh?"

"You know it ain't like dat;" Pee responded, still unable to look me in the eye.

But it was exactly like that. I had been dealing with Pee, copping blow from him for the past two and a half months. Every week I would take the short trip from Richmond to D.C. to purchase several ounces. The couple of hundred dollar price difference was worth the short trip along with the fact that his shit was raw. Pee's stuff was uncut, never stepped on and it always came back gravy with plenty of extras. Sometimes, whenever he felt like it, Pee would even drive across the Woodrow Wilson Bridge into Virginia and meet me off an exit in Northern Virginia, thus making things easier for me. I never shorted Pee. I always bought him straight money and I never tried to get over on him. So why did he sit there that day and tell me that if I didn't sleep with him, he was going to stop looking out for me? Not only was he talking about raising his prices, he was threatening to cut me off completely.

"You know what I want," he continued. "When you ready to give it up, lemme know. Until then..." CLICK.

The sound of Pee unlocking the doors magnified and echoed throughout the coupe. He was signaling for me to carry my ass. I stuffed the nine ounces I had just copped from him in my pocket and slammed the car door with so much force that I nearly cracked the windows after I exited. That was the end of the transaction and our business rela-

9

tionship. It was also the last time I ever saw him, until today that is.

I can honestly say that I liked dealing with Pee but since he wasn't going to play with principals, I had no choice but to seek out a new connect. Granted we did meet in a nightclub, but I had never given Pee the impression that I wanted anything more than drugs from him. He just wasn't my type and even if he was, at that point in my life, I was not willing to cheat on Ty, my soulmate and highschool sweetheart. From day one, I never played any mind games with Pee. He knew my name, Moe; Money Ova Everything.

Seeing Pee here today is causing me to relive the struggle I went through trying to find a new connect. The year was 1999 and the fact of the matter was niggas had a lot of garbage for sale. Nobody that I knew was giving up any raw powder and if they were, you were going to pay out the ass for it. I was spending my little money with different dudes but, no one was giving me the quality, consistency, or price that I was looking for. Earlier that summer, I had moved out of my mom's house and into my very first apartment. Bills were piling up on me and I was putting my whip game to the test by copping garbage ass coke and trying to turn it into bum ass flave. The bottom line was something had to give.

My baby Ty had tried on several occasions to hook me up with some of his boys that he knew fucked around but everything they had to offer was already cooked up and there was no way I was going that route. That's like buying a shoe box and hoping that the shoes inside are your size. I barely had ten thousand dollars that I could call my own and I was at a point where one bad re-up could take me out the game. But Ty still tried hard to help me out. At first all he wanted was for me to have what I wanted. All I wanted to do was make money and in the beginning that's just what Ty encouraged.

"Suttin' will shake sooner or later," he would say. "You can't appreciate the good without the bad. No storm lasts forever." And how could I forget his favorite words of advice? "Just don't forget me when you blow."

"Never," I would always answer, looking him straight in the eye and meaning it from the bottom of my heart.

From the first time I ever laid eyes on Ty, I believed he was my soulmate. In ninth grade, he stood six feet tall and was already carrying himself like a grown man. It was the first day of school and I was standing outside of my homeroom fiddling with the combination to my locker. I had been standing there a full three minutes unable to figure out why I couldn't get the damn thing open.

"Damn!" I slammed my palm on the locker, causing a mini-disturbance for no one in particular. That's when Ty came up behind me with a strong voice, full of attitude and annoyance.

"Hey, what the hell is your problem?"

I spun around ready to give him a piece of my mind. When we locked eyes, both of our nasty attitudes disappeared faster than sand in the wind. He wasn't the most handsome man I ever had the pleasure of being in the presence of, still. I saw something special in his eyes. He took a step back, as if the sight of my face took him by so much of a surprise that he needed to distance himself. The few seconds that we stood silence, eyeing one another seemed like hours. I saw a twinkle in his eye that day in the hallway of George Wythe High School. I assume it was the same twinkle one sees when staring into the eye of their soulmate, or their murderer, or the person who will make them very rich.

"What are you doin'?" Ty had rephrased his question and softened his approach. I swallowed deep and hard before I opened my mouth to speak. For some reason, at that moment my tongue was feeling like sandpaper.

"What does it look like I'm doin'?" I asked in a matter that was smart, sexy and sassy- all rolled into one, and then I whipped my head around ending his hypnotizing gaze. I was giving the lock one last try, when Ty stepped forward and closed the gap between us.

"Let me try." I took my hands off the dial and turned to face him so that I could tell him just what I thought of his suggestion but he was already reaching for the lock and turning the dial to the right.

"What do you think, I'm stupid? I'm not gonna give you my combination. I don't need ya help."

Just then the bell rang, signaling the end of homeroom and the beginning of first period. POP. He had opened my lock! There was no way he could have known my combination. The only place I had it written down was on the inside of my notebook. And then he looked at me with the cutest smirk on his face.

"How did you do that?" I demanded, thinking that I had just witnessed a magic trick of some sort. He ignored me, turned his back, turned the corner and was off down the hallway. I didn't find out until he sat beside me in our third period science class that I was trying to gain entry to the wrong locker. Ty's locker just so happened to be beside mine. The reason I was having such a hard time was because I was fiddling with his lock instead of my own. Yeah, I have to admit, Ty made a fool of me from the very start. That should have been a clear warning of what was to come.

Ty and I were deep in love by the fall break of our freshman year. At least, I was deep in love with Ty. I'm in no position to speak on the love Ty may or may not have had for me. We shared homeroom, two classes, a lunch table, and countless weekends together. By Christmas he was the owner of my heart and my virginity. During those first few years we shared an innocent love that pumped through our veins and felt just as necessary as the air we breathed. You couldn't have paid me to believe that things would have turned out the way they did.

Speaking of money, things eventually started to get better for me. It is always the darkest before the dawn and just between me and you, things were extremely dark for a minute there. One day, Ty and I had returned home from Kings Dominion and we were welcomed by complete darkness.

"I thought I gave you the money for the light bill last week sometime?"

"You said that was for the cable," Ty lied with a straight face while fumbling to find a flashlight. Whenever the bills were due, I would always give Ty the money and he would make sure they got paid. I had gradually assumed the role overtime, since Ty always had a hard time finding one job and sticking with it. He had quit a perfectly good job at the Wal-Mart warehouse but he was fired because of a dispute between himself and another employee. Before that incident he was working for UPS but was fired from there after a truckload of electronics came up missing. He hadn't had a job in over four months and money was getting tight, putting a strain on otherwise satisfactory romance.

"Ty, I'm positive that I told you to take that money and pay the light bill!" I shouted. Ty flicked on the flashlight and sat it on top of the counter.

"Help me find some candles. I'll go and get the bill so that you can see that it ain't been paid."

"Ty, I don't need to see the bill to see that it ain't been paid. The lights are cut off. You think I don't know you ain't paid the bill?"

He could act so stupid sometimes. I ended up having to go down to Virginia Power the following morning to pay the bill myself. As it turned out, the bill hadn't been paid in three months. I never found out what Ty was doing with the money I had been giving him for the light bill. I could only guess. That night, I slept under the candlelight; mad at Ty, with a heart full of hatred for Pee. That's when I realized it was me against the world.

The very next day my life took a turn for the better, or so I thought. For weeks prior, I had been holding tight to my dollars and praying for someone who would play fair with their prices. Between household bills and two unexpected abortions, my money was getting shorter and shorter. Before long, I wouldn't have anything to spend if someone didn't come along with some decent prices. But you know what they say. They say you never find the best connects, the best connects always find you.

I was on the way home from Ray-Ray's gambling spot. A lot of us would go to Ray-Ray's just to drink, gamble, smoke, gossip, pass the word, or wait on a sale. Some people just liked to be seen there. Ray's-Ray's place was a local meeting spot and that's just what I was trying to do there that night; meet me a new connect. When I realized there wasn't nuttin' shakin' in dat joint, I left and hopped on the highway, heading home. It was a little after one o'clock in the morning.

I was on the Chippenham Parkway when I saw a little white Honda Civic pulled onto the shoulder with flashing hazards. I looked. I don't know why I looked. I always look when I see a car with emergency lights on. Maybe it was the Good Samaritan in me. Or could it be the nosey person I am? Who knows? There was a young girl holding a baby and leaning up under the hood of the car. I couldn't help but notice the danger of her situation. I kept driving. There was about half a mile before the next exit. I drove and thought of the baby I had just paid to have murdered. I wondered if I were stranded on the side of the road, would anyone be kind enough to stop for me? If they did stop, what would their intentions be? I got off at the next exit and went back to help the stranded girl and her young child.

When I pulled up behind her I could see that she was squinting her eyes, affected by my headlights and trying to decipher the driver of my car. She was scared, just as I would be. As a matter of fact, I *was* scared. I had my trusted baby Glock on me and just my luck some asshole cop would show up, snooping around taking his job way too seriously.

"Are you okay?" I got out of my J30, cell phone in hand, and approached the skinny, Spanish girl.

"Me car no start," she cried in a Deep South American accent. As I got closer, I was able to see that the baby she had clutched to her hip was an adorable little girl who could have not been more than two years old. "It go boom..., boom, and then it just cut off," she dramatized to me the failure of her transmission. I could tell the girl was pleased to see that I was a female who didn't appear to have harmful intentions but at the same time she had rightfully assumed that I knew just as much about what happens under the hood of a car as she did.

"I saw you with the baby, so I stopped," I offered.

"Gracias. Gracias so much, senora. Can I use your telephono to call my Uncle or my brother?"

"Sure," I answered with a smile, pleased to hear that she hadn't asked to call the police. I would have let her dial 911 from my phone but as soon as she hung up with them I would have had to pull off. She called her brother and he was pulling up behind us within fifteen minutes to pick her up.

"Thank you so much for waiting here with my little niece and my sister," her brother Paco told me after the girls were safely inside of his Jeep Cherokee. "I always tell my sister I don't know how long she thinks this piece of junk car was gonna last her." I laughed lightly. Paco seemed cool right from the start.

"I don't know what would have happened to them if you weren't nice enough to pull over when you saw them. We all know that there are some real crazy people out here. Thank you, mami." Paco reached in his pocket and pulled out a fifty-dollar bill. "This is for your trouble," he offered.

"Oh no," I can remember the rejection clearly. I was going broke but I was not about to take fifty dollars from a stranger as payment for a good deed. "I was just doin' a good deed. I hope one day if I'm stuck on the side of the road someone will stop for me." He smiled. "Do you have any kids?" he asked. I felt like he was getting too personal so I cut the conversation short and started walking towards my car. To this day, I always thought Paco had a little crush on me. "Thanks again, mami," he said then waited for me to pull off before getting in his car and doing the same.

The next morning I received a call from a 305 area code.

"Yo," I answered, picking at the cold in my eye.

"Mami, this is the guy from last night. You helped my sister on the side of the road. You remember?"

I jumped up out of my sleeping position. I thought I had a real psycho type stalker on my hands. *That's what I get for helping people,* I had thought.

"Yes, I remember."

"Yeah, your number was in my phone from last night and when I told my uncle what a nice girl you were, he said that we should take you to lunch today."

"Oh, no thank you." Again I had declined his generosity.

"Nonsense. You must let me pay you back. You will come to our restaurant this afternoon. You turned down my money, at least let me feed you."

"Oh, okay," I gave in still half sleep. "What's the name

of the restaurant?" He gave me the name of the restaurant as well as the location and told me that he and his uncle would be expecting me at one o'clock. As it got closer to one o'clock, I thought about not showing up. Looking back, I can honestly say the only reason that I did go was because I did not want this Paco person to think that he had any reason to call my phone again.

I arrived in an orange and white floral sundress and a pair of peach mules. I fit in with the décor of the rather large and well-kept Mexican restaurant that Paco and his family owned. Paco greeted me at the door, and escorted me to a booth towards the back of the restaurant and then went behind the bar and made me a mango daiquiri. I felt comfortable in the restaurant. There was a family type atmosphere. Paco bought me my drink and informed me for a second time that his Uncle wanted to meet me. He left me with a menu and told me that he would be back shortly to personally take my order. When Paco returned he had an older looking gentleman with him and a drink of his own. They both took a seat opposite me at my booth.

"Senora," the older gentleman introduced himself. "I am Uncle Louie but, everyone just calls me Uncle," he smiled revealing a set of yellow chipped teeth that peeked through his salt and pepper mustache.

"Hi, my name is Moe," I smiled back, returning his firm handshake.

"Moe, so nice what you do last night. You know, my niece sat on the side of road for almost an hour before anyone stopped to help her. She's out buying a cell phone now," he laughed again. When I first met Uncle, I couldn't help but notice how happy he seemed. He was always laughing and smiling even when things weren't all that funny.

"That's a good idea," I said and then began to look down at the menu. Something about the attention both men were giving me made me a little nervous. Sensing that, Paco excused himself from the booth and walked back into the kitchen area.

"Yes, you look, and please order anything that you want from our menu. My wife is a great cook and she is gonna make your selection extra special today," Uncle smiled then leaned in lowering his voice before continuing. "So, tell me Moe. What is it that you do for a living? Paco tells me you turned down his money yesterday. I was surprised to hear that. I say "who is this woman who turns down fifty dollars?" Maybe she have rich boyfriend she want to introduce me to." Uncle leaned in further with yet another smile.

DING! Right then and there the light bulb went on in my head. I looked around at my surroundings and began to look at things from a different perspective. I fell right into place. "No, my boyfriend is not rich. I just did a good deed and didn't think that I deserved to be paid for it. I did it out of the kindness of my heart and like I told your nephew, I hope that if my car breaks down one day maybe someone would be nice enough to stop for me. I'm not rich but fifty dollars... I don't need your fifty dollars," I responded, mirroring his image with a smile.

Uncle respected my honesty. We talked about good deeds, karma, and money. Paco came back to the table and I ordered a shrimp chimichanga. He left and Uncle and I continued our conversation. I started to get slick with my tongue. I could see that Uncle was cool. "I'm just tryna put stuff together so that one day I can own a restaurant like this. I'm a hellava cook, you know. I been making money off my cooking for so long, it's only right that I start making some real money off of it." Uncle wasn't slow. He knew exactly what kind of cooking I was talking about. He looked around to see if anyone else had heard but there was no one else within earshot. His eyes grew with interest as I continued. "I'm not tryna get rich in this thing. I'm a fair person. I play by the rules. I just want what's mine and then I'm out. I know people. I been living in this city all my life and I know the right people. I just can't get my hands... I just can't get my hands on nuttin' good." Uncle was hanging on my every word as if I was giving him the next day's winning lotto numbers.

"Somethin' good, you say? Somethin' good," he smiled. Uncle had something good all right and pretty soon, I would too.

That's right around the time when my life started to change. Up until that day, I was a small time hustler, out there stepping on a few toes and trying to keep my head above water and my work on the street. I didn't have anything of spectacular quality to offer but I did work hard and I knew a lot of people who had decent amounts of money to spend. I didn't have anything for them to spend it on. That is until I met Uncle. After a few months of working with Uncle, I was getting more money than I had time to count.

Things were really changing for me and Ty was the first person to notice. The money was making me treat him differently. It wasn't a purposeful effort; it was just something that came naturally. I guess you could say it came with the territory. I could no longer trust Ty. Now don't get me wrong. I trusted him as a person. As a matter of fact, he was the only person that I could trust but what I didn't trust was his judgement. All of the heat my name was attracting in the streets began to melt away Ty's cool exterior. I moved to the front line, but he was growing tired of playing in the background.

"I thought we were going to D.C. today."

"Not today. I gotta take care of suttin' today."

I had less and less time to spend with Ty. It's not that I was falling out of love, I loved him more than ever, I was just busy. Uncle was giving me twenty keys a month and I was finished running the streets all day, the most I wanted to do was lay around the house, maybe have a little sex, watch a movie; you know, the things that ordinary people do. I could tell that Ty was missing having me around all the time. "You always got suttin' to take care of. It's like you always too busy for me," he complained. I looked at Ty and secretly wished that he did not depend on me as much as he did. I silently resented the fact that he spent my money without enduring any of the risks that I went through to make it. And then, he had the audacity to tell me that I wasn't spending enough time with him. I wonder why I had no extra time?

I could remember clearly me having to school Ty day after day. "Never drive straight home. Always take a detour, make a stop, and keep a check on your rearview." "Be careful who you are in the company of, we don't need to be meeting any new people." "Question everything, there is no such thing as a coincidence," I would always warn him. He would always reply in the same manner. "I got you," he would say.

There were so many nights I couldn't sleep because Ty hadn't returned home. Whenever he came home after me, I would have to stay up and make sure that he got in safely. How could I sleep knowing that he was still out in the street? Anything is possible and everyone knew that Ty and I were shacking up. The chance of someone using him to get to me was great. I carried a gun on a daily basis, that was a given. There were nights when I would come home and Ty's gun would still be in our nightstand and he would be nowhere to be found. How could I rest like that?

Even now as I lay here looking back on things, I can't say that Ty was a loser. Perhaps he did love me. But, the problem was I loved money. I loved him but, I loved money more. I mean, I would much rather stay at home, keeping the house clean, cook dinner, have kids, and that type of thing. But if I did who would see that the bills got paid? Who would buy me all of the things I wanted and felt like I needed. I've always been independent and I think Ty began to take advantage and at the same time find comfort in my independence. He began to feel like, "if she's gonna go out and do it, why should I?"

The day we argued about me not feeling like going to D.C. was the same day that Ty asked me for some work so that he could go out and make some money of his own. He had always dropped hints in that direction but that was the first day that he actually voiced his yearning to hit the streets. Why would he want to do something like that? Anything that he wanted to buy, he could have asked me for. Some of his boys were starting to tease him about the fact that his woman took care of him and I think that at that point it was starting to have an affect on him. I didn't want Ty to feel like he was one hundred percent dependent upon me but at the same time, I was not about to give him any work. I just couldn't do it.

"You go out here and give work to all of these different niggas that call your phone, but I'm living right here in your house. You sleep wit' me every night and you can't look out for me? I'm not askin' you to feed me! Just give me the food, I'll feed myself." Ty was furious. I was, too. This was truly the turning point in our relationship.

"Baby, I don't mind feeding you," I tried to explain my side of the story. "But if I give you work, where are you gonna keep it? You can't keep it here. I don't keep nuttin' up in here. This is where we sleep. And who are you gonna sell it to? Don't you understand that niggas will set you up just to get to me? It's too much of a headache. I don't need you out there doing the same thing that I'm trying to do. Where's the sense in that?"

Ty had no understanding as to what I was trying to say. "Oh so you the only one in the house that can get money?"

I could see that he was pissed off but, I didn't care. I had rules and I knew better than to break them. There would be no mixing of business and pleasure. If I gave Ty the key that he was asking for and he went out and messed it up, then what? What could I do? What if someone robbed him for it? What could I do? I wasn't going to make any money off of him so what was the point? I loved Ty and that is why I didn't want him involved in the game. He just couldn't understand that.

"I'm not sayin' that I'm the only one who can get money but I have enough money for both of us. Why do you have to go out there and try your hand for?" I asked sweetly in an attempt to smooth things over. "Cuz it's my hand!!!" Ty screamed, slamming the door as he stormed out of our apartment.

We were drifting apart. I never let Ty know exactly how much I was getting or who I was getting it from or any other particulars involving my business. The less he knew the better. I loved him and I trusted him but I hoped that I would never have to put that trust to the test. I was with Ty when I was just a regular broke girl, so I was sure that he loved me for me. After I started getting rich, serving half the town, there was no way that I could meet a stranger and then welcome them into my world. I was already familiar with Ty and I knew what to expect from him, so I decided to keep him. He is the only one who knew the real reason behind why I decided to get in the game in the first place.

Ever since I was fourteen years old, I felt like the drug game owed me something. My best friend, Noreen, introduced me to the world of high stakes and fast money. Noreen and I were the best of friends since middle school and we were given the chance to share two years of high school together as well. When I lost my virginity, Noreen was the first and only person that I told about it. Noreen had lost her virginity to a guy named Lo. Lo didn't go to school with us but he had an apartment in the projects directly across the street from our school. Noreen met him one day when we were cutting school and ever since that day they were inseparable.

Even I have to admit, Noreen and Lo did make a cute couple. They were the same honey-blonde complexion. Lo was kind of stocky and Noreen was kind of on the chubby side. Well, one day Noreen had cut school and was over Lo's house when some stick-up kids snuck in threw an open window and robbed the place. Lo didn't have a lot of money but he did have a big Cadillac and that was enough to convince watchful eyes that he was sitting on a gold mine. Noreen didn't survive the gun fire that, as she slept, she never saw coming. Lo was able to wake up and fire a few shots back but, it was no use. The three robbers were well prepared and they made off with a few grams of crack, a couple of thousand dollars and the keys to Lo's Cadillac.

My best friend, Noreen never sold drugs a day in her life. She never put anyone's life in jeopardy but yet her life was taken just the same. Sure Lo bought her nice clothes and kept her hair and nails done but did she deserve to pay for those things with her life? I was just so happy to see Noreen looking better and feeling good, I didn't think to warn her of the lifestyle her boyfriend was leading. I didn't know any better and by the time I did start to form an opinion on the situation, it was too late. My best friend was gone. I learned a lot from Noreen. I learned that if you're gonna die in a fire, it may as well be your food on the stove. No sense in dying over someone else's meal. I learned that it doesn't pay to have someone do for you what you can do for yourself. I got a lot of my independence from Noreen. Sometimes when I am really quiet I can hear her saying, "that's right Moe; milk this game for all it's worth." Noreen would want me to get money off the same lifestyle that ended her existence. Now, I had a dead president for every memory of my dead best friend and that still wasn't enough.

That day, when Ty left out of the house after our argument, I could remember thinking how I didn't care whether or not he came back. He was always whining. He encouraged me to find a good connect and make moves towards fortune but, it seems that he never thought that I would be as successful as I ended up being. I had moved my mom into her own condo in Baltimore. I had paid my favorite cousin's rent up for two years and put her in a new car. My brother's tuition at VCU was paid for; I'm talking about all four years. I had a Porsche 9-11 that I kept covered and parked in the backyard of me and Ty's quarter of a million dollar house. I had minks, leathers, stiletto, pumps, rings and things for days. I could go a whole month and never wear the same thousand dollar pocketbook twice. And look at me now.

I tell you one thing, I never thought that it would have went down the way that it did. No sir, if you had asked me, I thought it would have been the stick-up on I-95. Yeah, I would have bet anything that would have done it for me. I guess in some ways it was.

It was late, real late, about three thirty in the morning. So, I'm coming from Ray Ray's where I'd just lost a little under twenty thousand dollars. Eighteen thousand seven hundred to be exact. That damn deuce twice, it'll get you every time. I'm on the highway pissed off. It wasn't about the money. It was the fact that I had lost it to another female. Peaches, she always made me sick. Her nickel and dime, always tryna get over on some body, slick talking ass. Yeah, Peaches had money. She owned a beauty parlor, sold bootleg designer shit, and made a killing off of homemade porno movies. I even heard that she had a couple of hoes working for her. I wasn't mad at Peaches. I let her stand right there and beat me out my money. She was steady talking shit the whole time. "I know Mo Money ain't bout to quit. Shit. Mo Money got more money than all us. I know Mo Money ain't bout to quit." I always hated when people called me 'Mo Money'. Peaches knew just what to say to edge me on and I stood right there and let her talk me up on an ass whipping.

But I wasn't mad at Peaches. The dice were just in her favor that night. How could I be mad at her for that? I was mad at myself for gambling with her in the first place. Unless I'm out of town, I rarely gamble big money with someone who doesn't spend big money with me. Whether they go through someone else or they spend their money with me directly, even if I lose, I knew that I would get the money back. I was serving damn near everybody that gambled at Ray Ray's and if someone was lucky enough to beat me out of some real money, I could rest assure that my phone would be ringing early the following morning and they would be calling to give me my money back. See, but Peaches didn't get down like that. She wasn't in the drug trade, so my money was good as gone. I later heard that she fucked around and opened up another shop off of my money. The bitch had the nerve to call the place 'Mo Styles'.

So anyway, I'm pissed off driving down Interstate 95 on the way home. I'm so into my thoughts and in the process of sucking up my loss, that I don't even realize that I had been tailgating a Dodge Intrepid. When I finally got out of my daze, I saw that the car had Florida tags and was driving exactly fifty-five miles per hour. Upon closer examination, I noticed that the driver was a young white girl, who was wearing lots of cheap gold-looking jewelry. When I pulled up beside her so that I could finally get pass her that was the first thing that I noticed; all of that cheap jewelry.

Instincts are a motherfucker. I thought of my instincts

and how they had caused me to pull over the night I ran across the young Spanish girl on the side of the road. Tonight, I was not thinking about being a Good Samaritan. I was in vengeance mode and ready to take my anger out on some-body, anybody.

I slowed up and pulled behind the Intrepid for a sec-ond time and started tailgating again. The poor girl was driv-ing so cautious; she may as well have had the word 'trans-porter' spray painted across her back window. I had been in the game enough. Sometimes, I could even spot a mule driv-ing on the other side of the highway. I was just that obser-vant. I was tailgating her so close that I was only seconds from crashing into her but I was pissed off and didn't really care. The stupid girl pressed on her brakes, causing the crash bars of my Denali to collide with the bumper of her rental car. She still had the yellow Triangle sticker in plain view for all to see.

I don't even know why I did what I did. I can't say whether it was the fact that I wanted to ruin someone's night simply because mine had been ruined. Or maybe because I really wanted to discover the reason behind this young girl being on I-95 in the middle of the night, alone and driving the exact speed limit. Curiosity kills.

The girl slammed on her brakes and did exactly what I expected her to do. She pulled onto the shoulder. I pulled right behind her and hopped out, gun in waist. "What the fuck?" she shouted in a valley girl sort of way.

"If you wasn't driving so slow!" I shouted back.

It was pitch black and kind of chilly out. The only peo-ple out that time of night were truckers and people who were up to no good. "I'm gonna need to see your license and some type of insurance information," I continued with my charade. From the look on her face you could tell that the girl did not want me to get technical with her. She was busy assessing the condition of the vehicle and deciding whether or not it could still be driven to her destination.

"I don't have that far to go, just a few more exits. This isn't even my car so I won't sue you, if that's what you're thinking. We can just keep this between me and you. I'll get some- body to pay for any damage to your truck," she pleaded. I could see her cheeks reddening and she kept gripping her forehead out of nervousness.

The girl had said too much and just what I wanted to hear. But if she really only had a few more exits to go then maybe I was wrong about her. I started to think that I was standing on the side of the highway for nothing. There was only one way to find out. "Well, I'll just call the police. They can get to the bottom of this." I started to turn back as if I was going to my truck to get a cell phone.

"NOOOO!!!" the girl screamed as if I already had my gun drawn. It was music to my ears. I whirled around and took off like an Olympic track star at the start of a race, then pulled my Glock from out of my waist and pointed it at her frail body.

"Pop the trunk," I demanded.

"Who are you?" she cried with a confused look on her face. Her expression let me know that I was on to some- thing.

"Pop the trunk," I repeated. "Don't let me have to say it again."

"Don't shoot. Just take it. Please don't kill me," she begged for her life then opened the driver's side door and popped the trunk. With every step she took, my Glock was right there aimed at her head. There were two black suitcas- es in the trunk of the car. "Which one is it?" I asked the girl not expecting to see two suitcases. Whenever I had hired a transporter I would always have them put their clothes and the drugs and everything all in one suitcase. The girl pointed to the suitcase on the left, so I quickly unzipped the one on the right. BINGO. My heart skipped a beat when I saw the wrapped up packages. It looked just like the bricks of raw I had been getting from Uncle. The suitcase on the left was filled with nothing but clothes and shoes and I took that one as well. When both of the bags were in the back of my truck, I rushed back over to the girl. She was crying hysterically. I had to get out of there fast because I was now in possession of the drugs. At the same time, I started to feel sorry for the unlucky girl. I had no intention on killing her or being the cause of her death.

"You already lied to me once. Now, gimme your pocketbook. I don't have time to waste. I will blow your head off right here on the side of the highway!" She was stricken with fear. As expected, the girl did as she was told. She did not disappoint me, when I reached into her pocketbook and found a box cutter. Every female who thinks she's gangsta keeps one in her purse. I stabbed deep into her back left tire. It was just enough for the air to seep out slowly. I slung her pocketbook across my shoulder, keeping everything except her cell phone. That I threw on the floor and when she bent down to reach for it, I stepped on her little fingers then looked her straight in the eye.

"Now, listen here. I'm gonna let you live. If you mention me, my face, or that truck to anyone, I'm gonna kill whoever the person is who rented this car for you. I'm gonna kill whoever lives at the address listed on your license and any other address or phone number that I find in this cheap little purse of yours. You don't wanna fuck wit' me! I saved your life. The way you were driving, it was just a matter of time before the cops pulled you over." I then demanded for her to remove all of her jewelry and pass it over to me. The girl was petrified for her life and did exactly as she was told.

"Whoever shit you was carrying; you tell them that

your tire went flat. Tell them that somebody banged into the back of you. Call them right now and then call them back in five minutes and tell them that you got robbed. If you tell them anything different then that, they will kill you and if they don't, I will." SLAM. I smacked her across the face with my gun but not hard enough to draw blood and then I stepped off of her fingers and the scene.

I drove straight to one of my stash apartments. Not even Ty knew the location of this joint. This place was strictly my kitchen, I did nothing but cooking there. I could remember screaming and cheering myself on the whole way there. All I kept thinking was 'I wonder how many keys are back there?' Then I kept thinking 'what if that little bitch remembers my license plate?' I had made sure that she wouldn't be looking at my plates when I drove off. That blow to the face was enough to guarantee that. I carried the heavy bag into the apartment and dumped its contents onto my kitchen floor, 25 kilos. Free money and there was no turning back.

Imagine my surprise when a few days after the highway heist, Uncle called to tell me that he needed to see me. I didn't usually see Uncle until I was finish selling all of his work. I was in the process of waiting for him to bring me some more work so I couldn't figure out why he wanted to meet with me. The night of the heist, when I had opened up my free keys and began to cook them up, I couldn't help but notice the resemblance between the keys that I had stolen and the keys that I would get from Uncle once a month. Then again, I had never gotten keys from anyone other than Uncle, so far all I knew maybe all keys looked the same. Still going into the restaurant that day, I knew that something was up. There is no such thing as a coincidence. "Senora, have a seat," Uncle ushered me in.

There was no sign of Paco, which kind of threw me off. Every time I came to the restaurant, I always saw Paco, but not that day.

"Whassup," I greeted him, trying to remain cool. I had on a red Bob Marley t-shirt and my nervousness was beginning to form in puddles under my armpits. "I didn't expect to see you for another week or two." Boy, was I fronting. I felt invisible, like Uncle could see right through me.

"Something has come up," he announced, looking me straight in the face. I remember thinking 'am I blinking too much?' For some reason, I couldn't stop blinking and give him the eye contact he was looking for. There was just too much pressure.

"Something like what?"

"We have been robbed."

Those four words hit me like a Mack truck and I felt like the walls were closing in on me.

"What happened?" I asked. I should have acted more surprised.

As it turns out, the poor girl, who I had banged into on the highway and then robbed, was one of Uncle's couriers. Who would have thought? She wasn't lying when she said that she just had a few more exits to go. What were the chances of that? I had lost money, came up on a whole bunch of free money and now I was being told that I was about to lose money again. Due to the unexpected loss, Uncle was being forced to raise his prices. I would also have to wait a month or two before he would be able to give me any more work, that's if I was lucky. Supposedly, Uncle's people were threatening to cut him off now. When I stood on the shoulder of the highway that night with my foot on that girl's hand, I should have just shot myself in the foot because that is exactly what I ended up doing.

I was reckless. I had turned into a mad woman. I was mad at myself. I had jeopardized a year's worth of food for one big feast. There was no way that one feast could keep me fed. The fact that Uncle had been lying to me was the only thing that brought me to my senses and became a source of comfort for me. I was always under the impression that I was the only person that Uncle dealt with in this region. He told me this when I did not demand to know so I had believed him. Well, Uncle always delivered to me twenty keys, never more. So, why did I find twenty five keys in the bag that I stole from his courier? Uncle was going behind my back and giving work to someone else in this region. It was really none of my business but it was the only justification that I had for my actions. The body of the unlucky transporter was later discovered in the woods alongside the highway. I guess she wasn't a good liar.

With over half a million dollars of free blood money stashed away in three different places, I was beginning to recognize the need for my exit out of the game. I couldn't just pick up and disappear over night. I could but I would raise suspicion. I didn't know exactly how much Uncle and his people knew about their 'coincidental' misfortune. I had to play it cool and continue to press him about when he would be getting some more work. In the meantime, I had so much money in the streets that I knew niggas were talking and about to start testing me. I had so many people owing me so many thousands of dollars that I had to start writing it down just to keep track. When it gets to that point, you know you're in trouble because all it takes is for the wrong person to get their hands on that piece of paper and you could be going away for the rest of your life. I knew 'dem folks' had caught some type of whiff of my success and it was just a matter of time before they came with their bullshit indictments. Besides all of that, I was in the process of deciding whether or not I wanted Ty to continue with me on my journey through life. I had a lot of important decisions to make.

More and more, Ty was beginning to pressure me

about giving him some work of his own. I had been through too much in the past few weeks and the last thing that I needed was him causing unnecessary heat. If he wasn't asking about work, he was asking about when I was going to make him a father. The more I thought about it, the more I realized that I was ready to have children but first there were a few loose ends that needed tying. I had to collect all the money that I had out on the street. I had to play broke for a while and most importantly, I had to settle things between me and Ty. Although he didn't know very much, he knew more about my street life than anyone else and based on that alone, there was no way I was ready to part with him. At the same time I was growing tired of Ty's whining dependency. I began to feel like the only reason he wanted me pregnant was so that he could move my work in the streets being that I would no longer be in the position to do so.

Even a blind man could see that things were falling apart. I remember the moment when I realized that I had created a monster. Ty came home late one night, drunk and smelling like perfume. I didn't really wear perfume because so many of my hours were running the street and quite frankly I didn't care whether or not I smelled sweet. I actually preferred not to smell sweet. If people thought I was sweet, perhaps they would think about trying me. Anyway, as soon as Ty came in and I smelled him, I knew that he was doing something that he had no business doing.

Okay, so I cheated on Ty every now and then. He was my first and only for so many years and a girl can get bored with the same thing for so long. I needed a change and so there were a few occasions where I hooked up with this one or that one. 'Tip Drills' is what I liked to call them. No matter what I did, I was always smart and considerate enough to clean myself up before I came home. But in came Ty that dreadful night, reeking of another woman's perfume.

"Where you been?" I asked as he walked pass the living room sofa. He had that drunk eye with the sloppy stagger to match.

"I been out chillin' wit' my people. Look here, since you ain't gonna let me make no money wit' you, I'm gonna need you to give me some of my own." He really knew how to make a bad situation worse. There was no end to his bullshit. If it wasn't one thing, then it was another. I had just given him seventy five hundred dollars two weeks earlier and he was supposed to be using that money to start some type of car detailing service he had been researching. Now he wanted more money. The sad part about it was that he was dead serious.

"Money for what? Tell that bitch who sprayed her perfume all over you that you need some money. Don't tell me because I don't want to hear that shit." I spoke my peace and got up off the sofa, just as calm. I had been staying up waiting for his stankin' ass. Whenever he came home after me, I would always worry that maybe he had been followed. How do I know if he took all the precautions that I told him to take before coming home? There was always the chance of someone kidnapping him and forcing him to reveal where we lived.

"Oh, it's like dat, Moe? It's like dat?" Ty came staggering behind me. "You know what, Moe? Its ova. Its ova!!! I don't have to put up wit' dis bullshit!!! You go out all night and be around all type of niggas and as soon as I wanna go somewhere you throwin' the shit in my face and hangin' it ova my head. Fuck you, Moe!! Fuck you!!!" His words echoed. He was drunk and his words were coated with that drunken ring of truth. He was saying things that he wanted to say for years. He was mad at me. He was mad at me for being the breadwinner. He was mad at me for being as successful as I was. He was mad at me because the only thing that I needed from him was his companionship. He was mad because one day I would no longer need that and then he would be of no use to me. Was that my fault? Did I deserve to be punished? There was no more love between us, only harsh words exchanged.

Looking back on things, I should have left Ty right there at that very moment. I should have agreed with him and let the whole thing be over with. I should have just walked away from the house and let him keep all of that shit. If I was as tough as the image that I portrayed, I would have done just that. For some reason, I felt like I needed Ty. I needed the familiarity that his presence represented. I needed him around asking for my money so that I would feel needed myself. If I had broken up with Ty that night, how would I have known whether or not my new boyfriend was just with me for my money? I had so much money that it was impossible for me to trust a soul. Not a stranger, not a family member, and damn sure not a new lover. When it balled down to it, all I had was Ty and my money. How lonely would I be now that Ty was talking about leaving me?

I couldn't speak or respond to his outburst. We made love that night for the last time. Something inside of me should have told me that that was going to be the last time because the sex was absolutely incredible. I simply viewed it as good make-up sex and didn't think much of it. I was always in control in all areas of our relationship but when we ventured between the sheets, Ty enjoyed one hundred percent control. In the bedroom, I was at his complete mercy. The time we spent there was the only time that I willingly surrendered to his manhood. I let him take charge, set the pace, and the run the show. Some may think I was stupid to make love to Ty that night after he came home smelling like another chic but the truth of the matter was that I needed Ty, just as much as he needed me. I had gotten too big and it was Ty who kept me grounded. He helped me to remember where I had come from.

"How much money do you need?" I asked him in the midst of our post coital cuddling session.

"I saw this new medallion for my chain today. I want it," he whispered and kissed me on my neck

In many ways I had become the guy and Ty had become the girl. Things weren't always this way but, I had gotten to the point where I refused to play the background. I needed to see things being done and there was no better way to do that, than to actually get out and do it myself. My best friend had been killed playing the background. I was determined not to put myself in that same scenario. But what about those of us who step up and decide to play the front line? What consequences do we face?

"I don't have it like I used to. Ain't nothin' gonna come through for me for a while. We gonna have to cut back. I'm gonna have to go away for a while, maybe see if I can create a situation for myself elsewhere," I lied. I had more than enough money to relocate anywhere I wanted to and when I left I would never return.

I knew exactly what game Ty was playing with me. He was playing the 'if you wont let me make it for myself, I'm gonna make you wish you had' routine. Since I wasn't going to give him any work of his own, he was gonna drain my pockets until I got fed up and realized that perhaps he did need to start making money on his own.

"So, you leavin' me?" Ty knew me well. I had said 'I need to go away' rather than "we need to go away." He knew, just as well as I knew that this thing of ours was over. There was nothing left to salvage and even less to talk about.

"Why would you say that? I just gotta go away for a little while, decide my next move and come back with a clear head." I felt no need to tell him my genuine intentions.

Ty jumped up off the bed, naked, big dick hanging every-where. "I know you Moe. If I let you leave, you ain't comin' back. So if you think you leavin', you betta leave me wit' some work or suttin'. I know you don't think that you just gonna leave me here empty handed."

Ty was sick. The years of watching me do my thing had him sick with envy. I saw it a long time ago but I tried pacifying him with cash and material objects. If Ty had a dol-lar for every time he went somewhere and had to hear "tell ya girl to holla at me", he would be richer than me. I'm sure it hurt that he was labeled "Moe's man" but look at how many woman are satisfied being "so and so's girl". Is it not the same thing? I wanted for Ty everything that he wanted for himself but he could not have the things that I had already claimed. He was who he was and I was who I was. Money should not have changed that.

"What do you want from me, Ty?" I shouted at the top of my lungs, fed up." I want it all," he screamed as he stared at me with a strange look of death.

I knew at that point the break up would not be easy but, I had no idea that it would leave me in a casket. For the past four years, Ty had been using me but, what he failed to realize is that I had been using him as well. Somewhere along the line, he stopped being my better half and turned into the guy who kept my bed warm until I came home and got into it. Sad, but true. But what was even sadder was the fact that now that I was leaving, Ty began to realize just how little he had accomplished in the past few years. He couldn't deal with the reality of that and that last night in our house, he decided to take all of his pent up anger and jealousy out on me.

I want to be able to tell you that Ty and I went our separate ways peacefully, that day. I wish that I could tell you that I survived the game and that I lived to tell about it.

For so long, I thought that all that I wanted was money. I was under the impression that money could purchase happiness. All I wanted was to be happy. As I lay here today, I realize that I was happiest before I had any money at all. Look at me now.

So, this is what my funeral looks like. There are a lot of people here that I don't even know. I've never seen them before in my life. There's my mom in the front row. And look at my brother seated beside her. My cousins, all of my cousins, and my aunts and uncles. I guess you don't realize how much family you have until something bad happens. Who are those men in the back? I guess those are the Feds. I always knew that I'd have to see their faces one day. Wow, Noreen's mom is here and my hair dresser and that one girl who always speaks to me but I don't know her name. This is a pretty big turnout and everyone is dressed so nice, so dark but, so nice. And flowers, there are enough flowers here to start my own garden I feel so special. No one has ever bought me flowers before.

I wonder why my mom keeps turning around and looking at the back door. It's as if she is expecting someone. Who could she be expecting? Oh!!! It just dawned on me. She must be waiting for Ty to come. I wish I could jump out of this casket and let her know that he will not be showing up here. He is somewhere long gone, probably chilling and spending my money. I can't believe he went out like that. I can't believe that that one argument ended up like this. I knew things were getting bad between us but, I never in my wildest dreams thought that this would be the end result. Good thing he only got a hundred grand. The rest of my money is in my safe at my mom's house and in the stash box of my hoopty which is parked in my mom's backyard. I only hope that my mom doesn't get rid of that car before she looks around it a little. That would be such a disappointment.

I guess all in all, the funeral was a success. It was well attended by a lot of popular people and everyone seemed sad about my situation. I just wish that I could tell certain people certain last minute things. Like, I wouldn't mind telling my mother about the money that is at her house that she may never find. I wouldn't mind telling my brother and my favorite cousin that I love them and they should not cry for me. I am in a better place. I no longer have to worry about all that street-related stress that I was subjecting myself to. I can relax and let someone else take control instead of always being the aggressive decision maker. I just hope that I don't fade into the background too fast.

I always wondered what it would feel like to be my grandmother's age, old, wise, beautiful, and full of experience. I will never know what that feels like now. I lay here, dead at the age of 23. How did it happen? Where did I go wrong? If you ask me, I think it was the money. But, at this point, it doesn't really matter what I think. I'm just a regular Moe.

A.J. Rivers makes her debut in the literary career with that easy to follow, gripping page-turner "CASH MONEY" on Triple Crown Publications. She currently resides in Central Virginia, where she is hard at work on her second book. She can be contacted at morivers@comcast.net or P.O. Box 35180, Richmond, VA. 23235.

The Auction

Jasmin L. Harry|

Gemini DeVeaux was an erotic, intense, and mysterious woman. She was every man's fantasy, which helped to cast her as the main character. Her full grapefruit sized breasts seem to stand at attention no matter what the occasion or the weather. Her ass was magnetic. Every male and female eye watched her as she walked by, in some odd way they were attracted to it. A bevy of curled lashes engulf her piercing dark brown eyes as they manage to swallow anyone who dare to get close enough to gaze. The smooth lightly toasted caramel complexion adorns her 5'7" shapely hour glass stature. Move over Ms. Tina. There's a new Hanes girl in town.

It's in the power of her walk, the way her full naturally rose colored lips form as she speaks. It's the way the midnight blue curls cascade over her face. It's how her clothes embrace her form. She was a confident and beautiful woman, but she was not conceited. She totally embodies every insatiable inch of her womanhood. No one would believe that Gemini is forty years young.

Gemini owns and lives in a tightly furnished, 3 story brown stone located in the Clinton Hills section of Brooklyn. With 5 bedrooms, 3 baths, gorgeous hard wood floors, imported Italian furniture and captivating artwork, her place is fit for a Nubian queen. With her ice blue two door Jaguar parked in her private garage, she definitely has it going on. After becoming the Director of Finance and Marketing for her company, a sister could afford to live large.

Flashback: 2003 - Gemini has worked at Studio One, the largest architect firm in Brooklyn, for five years. She has gone from writing loans for different housing facilities and typing up various business documents to overseeing building projects as a manager. Over the years she has seen the many changes the company has undergone. The horizon was great.

Although never experiencing any prejudices because of gender or race, Gemini felt long overdue for a promotion. She diligently worked on various projects, always went past the call of duty on office assignments and often worked excruciating long hours. And getting laid didn't even happen in her dreams. In fact, most nights while riding the 5 train home after work, Gemini's wildest fantasies involved her naked voluptuousness body sprawled out... in bed under her covers buried deep within her pillows. It ain't a game. A sister was tired.

She consistently did good work, yet received minor compliments and "keep up the good work" from her boss. In Gemini's mind, compliments and soft pats on the back didn't pay the bills. However, Ms DeVeaux found her own way of climbing the corporate ladder.

Bring It Back: 2005 - It was Thursday the 24th of February, which only left four more days until the big lottery. It will take more than a dollar and a dream to win this particular lottery. On Monday, several contracting companies will have the opportunity to bid on the blue prints for Studio One's new billion dollar project. The architects at S.O. (Studio One) have spent months designing and developing a new high rise co-op equipped with the latest and finest advanced technology for the low moderate income level family. The city has approved funding for this project which is going to be a major breakthrough for the company.

Studio one needs the best contracting company to do the job and one willing to agree to the monetary terms set. Any contracting company lucky enough to win this auction will undoubtedly stand to be placed above the rest. Any other lottery would have been anticipated by Gemini, but something lay lingering on her mind; it all stemmed from two Fridays ago when Studio One first put out the word about the new project.

"Well Gemini, looks like this project is finally going to come together once we find a good enough contracting company," said Cynthia, a co-worker. It was 5:08 in the evening and the temperature was about 72 degrees. The two women spoke in Gemini's corner office which overlooked the Hudson River. Gemini spent many nights gazing out of her floor length windows at the sexy sunsets which looked like running colors from a canvas on a hot summer's night. "I know girl. Rich folks ain't gonna be the only ones living like kings and queens" responded Gemini as she sat back in her cream, lambskin swing chair fiddling with two paper clips.

Cynthia was a 27 year old, round faced, stocky woman who had been at Studio One no more than 2 years. She was a baby to the game and Gemini knew her kind all too well. She was your typical "go to" girl. Go to Cynthia and she'll do whatever you ask, especially if you're the CEO. Cynthia did everything in her power to please Mr. Ramos at no cost, even if it meant enduring brutal rug burns and bruising those chubby little knees of hers. Little did Ms. Cynthia know, but that shit would only bring her a messed up back and permanent lockjaw.

"You think with all the companies bidding, there will be one willing to agree to our financial terms?" asked Cynthia sitting on the red leather sofa adjacent to Gemini's desk, (still messing with the paper clips), "Cynthia this is the biggest job in New York's architectural history. Those contractors are going to be bidding their little hearts out; they'll practically be cutting each other's throats to get up on this offer. Our job is to pick the best company for the project."

Just then, Gemini was interrupted by the phone at the front desk; Cynthia ran to answer it. It was about 4 seconds before Cynthia called out to Gemini, "Call on line 4!" It was now 5:32. Gemini had a little under a half hour before she got off from work. She yelled back, "Cynthia, I'm about to be up out of here in 30. Who is it?" There was a pause before Cynthia yelled back, "It's David Green, he said he's an old friend and wants to holler at his girl!" David Green. Gemini's panties dampened at the mere mention of his name. "Ohhh girl, transfer....pa leeeez!" David had studied at Baruch with Gemini and she remembered his outrageous humor that got her through the bad times at school as well as his 10 inch cock that did the same.

Ring! "Hey Mr. Green! Long time, no hear!" The voice on the other end was deep and scruffy and sent the hairs on Gemini's neck into an erect position. "Ms DeVeaux, we speak again." Gemini knew the voice didn't belong to David Green, but rather to a person she had hoped never to talk to again ever in life. It was Christon Solomon, a 39 year old, dark skin, 6'1" smooth talking brother in the contracting business. About two years ago, this Morris Chestnut look alike gave Gemini a huge boost up the rungs of success.

Pause: Let's Take It Back -"Damn ma, what time you gone be done? I got to lock up," asked Lou in his cute Brooklyn Italian accent. With a mountain of papers on her desk, Gemini gave an exhausted reply, "You know me Lou. Gotta knock this shit out; report due first thing in the morning." Lou was the security guard and for the past couple of weeks, against company policy, he had been letting her lock up on her own after his shift was over. "Yo Gem, you know I got mad respect for you cuz yous a female doin ya thing and all but I gotta stop lettin you close the office. This shit here is my bread and butta. If I get caught...," said Lou. Gemini knew Lou spoke a true word but tonight was different. She needed to be alone in the office just this one last time.

Now standing directly in front of him, Gemini interrupted Lou, "Sweetie, you know I'm not gonna let that happen. Promise, this is the last time. This report has to be done before I leave tonight. This is my big break. When it goes to the board tomorrow, all these years will finally mean something and you know I got you papi." She playfully tugged on Lou's ears. Gemini had promised to get Lou a position in Studio's main office building once she got her promotion. Lou saw how hard Gemini had worked over the years he had been there and he especially saw how great her determination was over the past few days. And the fact that she was fine as hell and the way she tugged on his lobes helped him to tonight's final decision. "Here girl. Last time," he said reluctantly as he slipped the keys into her hand. Gemini winked, "Last time. Trust me."

Fuck it. If muthafuckas won't give me mine, I'm takin mine. These thoughts ran a marathon in Gemini's mind.

Earlier in the week, she had thought up tonight's plan that even shocked her. There are classified files containing information that only the CEO and board officials are privileged to; most of which are various figures and graphs outlining different future projects that the company would like to manifest sometime in the future.

Gemini, along with the other project managers, was given two weeks to come up with a full report outlining the scheme for a new project that would propel the company to new heights. The CEO wanted to see just how much initiative his employees would show toward this assignment and who was ready to take on an executive managerial position. This was Gemini's big opportunity to show Mr. Ramos and Studio One execs what she was capable of and how much she had learned over the years. This was her time to shine above the rest and take her rightful place in the company - on top.

After about a week and a half working on the report, Gemini became intensely frustrated. She would from time to time ask her colleagues how things were going with their reports. "Oh just fine," Sherman said. "This is the best opportunity, I'm so excited," Heather would cheese. Gemini would return the same phony ass answers she felt her co-workers were given her. But for some reason, Gemini couldn't help but feel they really did have shit under control. She was sweating fucking cannonballs. She was so busy trying to find out what her co-workers were devising in their reports and she wanted so badly to top them, that every idea she came up with just didn't seem like the right one. The hourglass neared its last grain. Desperate times called for desperate measures.

On this night in question, after Lou had gone, Gemini got right down to business. Getting into the system was a piece of cake for her. A couple of days ago, Gemini had

Clayton, the office's nerd and official ass licker, look up some documents on the server. She didn't really need these papers but it gave her an excuse to stand over his shoulder long enough to memorize the password he slowly typed into the mainframe.

This is too easy, she thought to herself as she entered into forbidden cyber territory. The password was a success; she easily gained access to the company's main files. Gemini became a little overwhelmed. "Damn. Look at all this shit. Why the hell they got us writing reports if they already have plans? Oh well. Studio One is about to blow up! And I'm lighting the muthafuckin stick of dynamite", she thought to herself. She felt like a straight gangsta. "Ok. Focus girlfriend. Get what you need and let's get the fuck out of here quick fast." Gemini skimmed over the various numbers and plans, printed out what she deemed useful and took an array of notes. Before she knew it, two hours had passed. "Time to get the hell up out of there" she thought. She would type up her report when she got home.

"Oh shit!" What the fuck just happened!? "Shit! Shit!" The screen went blue. As Gemini went to print out one last page before shutting down, she eagerly slammed down on the wrong key and accidentally erased data. Instantaneously, Gemini felt like a junkie trying to quit heroin, cold turkey. She began to sweat profusely and her mouth became drier than the Sahara. Fuck! Fuck! Fuck! She didn't know what to do.

Gemini worked out of Studio's smaller office space which was located on Nevins Street in a building shared by other companies. Someone happened to be going over some building plans in one of the offices located down the hall and around the corner from where Gemini was straight trippin. He needed some blue prints that were in an office two doors down from Studio One. On his way, he noticed the light. Before Gemini could think of an excuse, the glass door swung open. "What are you doing in here?" Gemini froze as if she could somehow make herself invisible and the man would just walk away. But that wasn't the case. "I asked you a question. What are doing in here this late?" asked the handsome stranger as he edged closer toward Gemini as she still sat motionless.

He came around to where she sat, close enough to see the computer screen. "I... I'm going over some d...d...documents," trembled Gemini. If it were ever found out that she was tampering with the main files of the company and managed to erase some of them, her career as she knew it would stop dead. She was facing termination, possible legal charges being brought against her and total humiliation. She couldn't let that happen.

Fortunately for Gemini, this was a clever man and he soon realized what she was up to; he fingered a few keys and the lost info magically reappeared on the monitor. With pea sized beads of sweat trickling down her forehead, Gemini let out a deep sigh of relief. She had her fix. "Thank you so much...but how?" she asked perplexed. "I took a few computer courses in college, but enough about me." he answered. "This office is usually closed at seven."

"Why don't you stop bull-shitting me and tell me the real reason you're in here," he asked with a certain glare in his eyes.

Gemini knew this man wouldn't believe any two bit lie she tried to think of, "Who are you anyway? Why are you here so late?" she asked with a hint of attitude. Before answering, he took the keyboard off the desk and up into his lap so he could sit down. Gemini's heart began to skip a bit as she couldn't help but take a glance at the fantastic bulge staring right at her from in between this stranger's legs. "Christon Solomon," as he took her hand into his. "I work for

Copeland Industries. I was going over some blueprints for the Mac Field project. And you're here trying to get which promotion?" The two stared into one another's eyes, for there was an immediate heated attraction.

"The promotion that includes the fabulous corner office next to the CEO's and the $70,000 a year salary," she quickly answered. It was as if the magnetism of his eyes had reached into her soul and brought forth the truth. Once again, Christon magically fingered some keys and erased some current data and replaced it with new information that would accelerate Gemini's career. She looked at the screen after he was done. "Shit! Those stats and figures are better than what was originally proposed by the execs. My boss is going to love that; Studio One will take this city by storm. How the fuck... ." Christon interrupted by placing his thick chocolate finger across her lips and explaining it would be their little secret. Gemini felt unusually and fearfully safe. At that moment, she lost all inhibitions. She touched his thigh and noticed his boy salute at full attention and right there, at her desk, she took him completely into her mouth. Not too long after their first meeting, she had reason to be fearful; Christon held the incident to her memory like a loaded gun. It had been about eight months since she heard from him.

Play: We're Back -"What the hell do you want?!" asked a seething Gemini. "Ohhh baby. No 'how are you Chris?' I'm shocked Gemini, you have better manners than that. So, when do you want to start going over the plans for the new project for Studio One." he asked with shrewdness. Just then, Cynthia walked in, "Gem, it's 5:45. I'm leaving. You want a ride?" Gemini took the phone from her ear and covered the mouthpiece, "Sure babe, let me just say good-bye. I'll meet you downstairs, okay?" Cynthia nodded. Gemini waited a few seconds, took a deep breath and spoke, "I have to go. Don't call back!" She hung up and left the office.

————— TWO WEEKS LATER —————

"Males and females, listen up! I am presently on my way to a meeting downtown. Please have your disposition packages prepared; it is now Friday and Monday we have a hectic schedule ahead of us. This place is going to be crawling with people," addressed Mr. Ramos. "Oh, uh, Cynthia! In my office. I need a memo drafted quickie. I mean quickly. Gemini, hold down the fort!"

All she could do was think about this man being back in her life and how to please him and keep her job at the same time. To meet Christon for the first time, you'd think he was a sweetheart who could lay it down like no other. But get to know him and it was shear torture, especially when he had something to hold over your head. He called Gemini's home all week long. She almost anticipated it. But would he listen to reason? Would he understand her point? The answer was NO.

"Look Gemini, it's been almost two years and you owe me...you owe me big! I'm ready to collect my dues," snarled a ruthless Christon. Gemini replied with nervousness and a bit of anger, "You've got some fucking nerve coming back into my life and demanding shit! I took care of you already. I..." Just then he interrupted, "Wait bitch! Don't get loud! You're in no position to become fucking superwoman. You took care of me? You took care of me?!! Hold the fuck up! Your pussy and ass was tight but that shit wasn't spitting out Benjamin Franklin's, love!" Christon took a breath and a slight moment to regain his composure, "I want what I want Gemini and I'm not taking no for an answer."

Gemini stood still for a minute. "Look Chris, you're just going to have to come to the lottery like all the other contractors. I'm more than willing to gather up for you a nice sum of money that..." The wicked laughter of Christon interrupted her sentence and broke her spirit, "You must be a fool! I happen to know that this new project can bring me in more money than you could ever imagine to gather up for me." All of a sudden, with a sly compassion in his voice, "Look Gem, don't play with me. I need to make this deal or I could lose my job. Copeland hasn't been doing too well and we might be going under. This deal would really help. Copeland gets this contract - we do the job - I get paid – and I'm out of your hair. Don't you care at all that I might end up on the streets somewhere?"

Gemini closed her eyes, inhaled slowly and exhaled in the same manner and spoke in a soft tone, "Chris, I'm sorry about Copeland but I can't...there's too much at stake. Copeland is a small company. Storefront buildings are cute but ya'll really haven't set a precedent of fabulous work around the city. In fact, Copeland is hardly heard of anymore. No matter what I say to Ramos, he ain't going for it. Like I said before, you'll have to bid along with the other companies and prove your company to be..." Christon interrupted. "Don't you remember baby? That first night.", and then he begins to drift down memory lane.

Cumming Attraction: The Flashback - The cramp in his right foot was severe as his toes curled to almost a backward position as he received the best head in all his sexual years. She stroked his shaft as if it were a piece of clay she was sculpting into a masterpiece. She took a second and looked at his throbbing member, spit down on it and deep-throated until her nose touched right below his bellybutton. Placing his hand on her head, he guided her fellatio strokes. As she slowly lifted her head from his cock, she playfully flickered her tongue over the head and then sucked on his plump balls.

Passion running wild, he gently grabbed her hair

and pulled her up. He then ripped open her silk blouse exposing those magnificent extra ripe melons. He sucked like a newborn clinging to its mother for the first time. Her nipples were so hard. As he kept one hand on her left breast, he used his right hand to go into Gemini's bare wetness. Her moan was long and it was deep.

In one motion, he took both of his hands and lifted her high and indulged in her neatly trimmed bush. He ate and ate and ate. Just the fact that he could lift her high enough to suck the juice straight out of her clit had Gemini almost going into cum-vulsions. She thought she was going to squeeze his head too tight as her legs automatically locked in place. Christon was a pro. He slowly and carefully walked away from her desk to a bit of open space. He knelt to the floor and placed Gemini on her back. Damn, her pussy was wet and fresh.

His shirt was open and Gemini saw his chiseled smooth black physique. She was ready for him to enter. He teased her clit with his tongue for a few seconds longer. He then looked into her eyes, took his tongue and licked all her juices from around his sexy lips. His shit was rock hard and ready for submission. 3, 2, 1....enter erogenous zone. In and out, and out and in he moved. Gemini moaned, "Fuck harder, now fuck slower, and now fuck me in the ass. I'm ready to explode. Open your mouth. Give it to me daddy.

Reality Check: The Present - Panties soaked, heart pounding and legs quivering, Gemini had to take a moment. Damn. She had almost forgotten how good it was that night and the few months that followed. With self control, Gemini responded. "That was a cute thought to remember. Look this is getting tired. I can't help you. Stop calling me or I'm going to get your ass for harassment. Don't fuck with me Chris."

"No bitch, don't fuck with me! You so fucking selfish, sitting on your little pedestal high and mighty. If it weren't for me, you'd probably be right where I found you - trying to find ways to come up. You ain't shit. I made you!" Gemini interrupted this time, "Nigga please! You might have typed in a few little numbers and shit but don't get it twisted. I made me. You were just a stupid muthafucka that did what you did cause you saw pussy. And you know the pussy was all that."

Christon Solomon - the first black man in history to actually turn red. He was getting fed up with her sudden Sista Souljah fearlessness and that slick mouth. He had a vendetta against her and he aimed to get even.

After submitting her report to The Board, she immediately moved up in the company. During the months it took for the execs to deliberate, Gemini and Christon had a torrid affair. They fucked anywhere. And they did everything in the book, even shit that hadn't been written yet. And then she got the promotion. Everything changed. She got bored with his ass and dropped him like a hot pot of grits. She changed her phone number and simply stopped all types of communication. Once he showed up at her new office and she had Lou escort him out. "LEAVE...ME...THE...FUCK...ALONE...I...DON'T...NEED...YOU!" These were the last words spoken between them until now.

He lay low for the past months and let Gemini bask in her sunshine but now was the perfect opportunity to put his plan to action. He longed for the moment to see Gemini wriggle like the snake he felt she had become.

"Gemini, my dear, go to your fax machine. I have a little something for you," said an insincere, cold-hearted man. She saw a fax coming through and put the receiver down on her desk and walked over to the machine. To her surprise, there was a letter and Xeroxed photos; the photos were of her at the computer on that dreadful night in question. The letter was addressed to Mr. Ramos explaining what happened two years ago. Gemini grabbed the lethal information and hurried back to her desk, "You bastard!"

But that wasn't all. "Oh wait, you should have a package delivered to your door soon," said Christon basking in his own glorious moment. Like clockwork, her secretary buzzed in, "Ms DeVeaux, you have a package." Gemini ran to open the door, grabbed the package and slammed the door in Linda's face. She opened it to find a videotape and a CD Rom. She turned on her television and the VCR and popped it in. Oh shit. Gemini fell to the floor. She suddenly became nauseous. She stopped and ejected the tape. She crawled back to her desk and took the phone to her ear, "You were there all the time."

Christon gave a laugh, "You look good baby. Don't you think? I know they say the camera adds ten pounds but your ass looks gooder than a muthafucka." The tape showed them having sex and the CD Rom contained two files - the original information on Studio One's mainframe at the other office and the information Christon replaced it with to help Gemini. "Now, if you don't want these things to end up in the wrong hands, you'll get me what I want. I'll see you Monday." Gemini felt so trapped, "This isn't fair Chris. How am..." The click of the phone interrupted her sentence. She just sat there and slowly put the receiver down.

Jasmin L. Harry was born and raised in Harlem, New York. She free-lances for BLOW! Magazine, with pieces already published in the first and second issues. She is currently finished her up coming novel "Twisted Gemini." She maintains life in Brooklyn with her son. Jasmin can be reached at Jasmin@Jacksonpress.net

CurtainCall

Felicia S. Rutty

Finally, the time I've anticipated has finally arrived. At that moment, I thought about how much one person is able to endure before they realize, it's all bullshit. I thought that love, money, family, friends, a great career, and great sex would bring me happiness, and it did for a long time. But now selfishness, regret and painful sorrow consumes my soul. I have said farewell to those doubtful morning, afternoon anxieties and midnight sorrows. Where I'm going there will be no more empty promises, fake smiles or boldfaced lies. There will be no soft whispers of I'm sorry or crocodile tears shed in July. No more handsome faces, pushing Benzes and Ranges convincing me that pain is pleasure and one day, if I'm patient I might be THE ONE. No more phone calls from her asking who am I and why is my number on her man's phone bill? No more embarrassment as I rush to an 8:00 dinner date to realize after two hours of waiting and a bottle of red wine that tonight, I will eat alone again.

I've tried shopping, food, alcohol, drugs, and sex, to try to hide my pain. If you can think of it I tried it. I've tried psychiatrists who medicated me, self help books put me to sleep, meditation only worked while I was meditating. I've consulted psychics, tarot cards and had my palm read. I even joined a church and thought that was the key, until I realized that the devil visited church too. He visited the pastor in the pulpit, the gay men in the choir and let's not forget the married men that would wink at me when their wives weren't looking. I was desperately searching for anything that would make sense of this bad luck or to take the curse away that was placed on me by my father. Is there another way? Is there another way to make the memories and heartache disappear?

After placing the razor on the edge of the tub, I had to choose the right candle. Which one would it be? Each had a story and chocolate was my favorite, so I reached over and lit the 6 chocolate candles given to me by a special friend. We agreed that they would only be lit on our first night together as we fed each other strawberries covered in white Godiva chocolate. I looked forward to that day, afternoon, night for 4 years now, imagining how it would be. What music would be playing in the background? How much champagne would we consume before our conversation got hot and steamy? Would he rub my feet, maybe I would giggle as he kissed each toe on my foot. Would he tell me something I wanted to hear or something I wanted to know? Stuff like his last name, his favorite dish or maybe share one of his childhood fears. After a few minutes of wondering I popped back into reality and knew we wouldn't make it to the tub. We'd tear off each others clothes in the foyer, start on the couch and if I was tactful we'd spend another 30 minutes hanging off the bed.

As I stood in front of the medicine chest, I took a long

stare at myself. I tilted my head back and swallowed the remaining pills in the bottle. As tears streamed down my face a smile arose. It was a smile of relief knowing that it would soon be over. There was only one determining factor that I pondered before making this choice. Would I be missed? I thought of all the people I knew. My mother, father, two sisters, my daughter, and her father they were the closest to me and I knew that they would feel some discomfort but time would heal their wounds, just as it always did in the past. Most of their concerns would be financial, the burial and all. So, I made sure to pay off all my debtors and deposit the rest of my funds into an account for my daughter. I stepped back from the sink; the coolness of the Italian marble titles sent a soft chill up my spine. I glanced down and reminisced on Marco and Juan as they laid each piece while sipping on a glass of Manzone, as I watched from the doorway. I could hear Ms.Thomas from apt 10-C complaining to the concierge about the noise accompanied by our drunken laughter.

My robe slid off my shoulders and to the floor. I took a last glance at the body I would never see again. Still slim and never a pound over 125, I admired my body for the first time, seeing what my lovers saw. A proportionate woman 34, 28, 36, skin colored a soft, smooth, honey brown with eyes to match. I unpinned my hair and watched it flow slowly down past my diamond studded ears, draping my shoulders and down my back. What a waste 3 visit's a week with a trainer at the gym, to sculpt these thighs. Spinning around I see my calves, show stoppers as the Manolo's kiss the New York City pavement. A soft brush across my breasts made me chuckle. I was always conscious about the size of my breasts, them being a 34A even after having a child. After 20 minutes of caressing, Roger would say "A mouthful is all a man needs" and then showed me what he meant. When I really thought about it my ass overcompensated for any short comings. It made me smile.

Left foot, right foot into the tub I sank. The warm water felt so good on my skin and the medicine began to numb my body. All it took was two little slices and off I would go. Slice number one, didn't feel as bad as I thought it would. Slice number two would be much easier. From the corner of my eye I could see that I had a spectator. He had the deepest black coat, perfectly shaped ears and solid auburn eyes to match. His eyes pierced through me and looked filled with tears as if he wanted to cry for me. He watched each move so intently. I would miss him. He was great company that very rarely ever left my side. He slept at the foot of my bed while I slept, sat on the dining table and watched me cook. He would greet me each morning when I used the bathroom, rubbing on my leg and purring with such satisfaction. It made me feel as if he was saying, "I'm glad you woke up this morning" or maybe his bowl was empty and he really wanted something to eat. Nevertheless he was always there, just as he is here now.

With slice number two I began to feel weak. My eyes shut ever so gently and images of familiar faces appeared. I could hear my favorite tunes and with my last few breaths, the sweetest smells filled my nostrils. I released all anger and all bitterness, frustration and regret, fears and disappointments. I was no longer sorry for the things I had done or the things people had did to me. I finally let go. It was finally over....

Felicia currently resides in Upstate New York where she continues to write poerty.

LIVE BY THE GUN

Shannon Holmes

The bitterly cold winter winds ripped through the streets of Washington, D.C., rendering it an absolute ghost town. Winter was in full effect. Even as the city endured these adverse weather conditions, it seemed eerily quiet, even for this time of night. One would be lucky to even spot some unfortunate soul walking to the corner store or 7/eleven, braving the elements. In fact, the city was so cold and silent it was as if even the killers had taken the night off. Imagine that. Somewhere within the city limits someone was either meeting their maker or about to.

After all this was Washington, D.C., Dodge City. This city had once held the dubious distinction of being the murder capital of the world. So surely somewhere a killer or killers were, practicing their craft, putting in work, taking someone off this earth. Because of the thriving drug trade, death was in the air, even on a night like this. Drama didn't take any days off.

On the streets there wasn't any sympathy, mercy or remorse. In light of the recent cocaine drought, dope boys turned to robbers and the real stick up kids were working overtime, looking for potential victims. Everyday one had to be on guard for their life, expecting the unexpected, especially if one were living on the other side of the law. Mike Jones was just that kind of person, an outlaw. He was going all out to get ahead in the rat race.

He zoomed through the streets of Washington, D.C, like a madman, in his brand new mustard yellow Nissan 300zx convertible, with a black top, temporarily shattering the serenity of the night.

Mike sped through the town, as if he owned the streets. To his dismay, there wasn't a cop in sight, so he pushed his five speed coupe to its limits, summoning all of the car's horsepower, racing up North Capitol Street. He hoped a cop car would come out the cut and give chase. But none did.

Mike and his girlfriend had just come from a Go-Go music show at the MCI center. He was still hyped up from the spirited performances of the local groups. The loud drum kicks and lyrics still echoed in his head. There was nothing like Go-Go music to get him overexcited.

Usually Mike reserved these high speed antics for when he was alone or on the Baltimore/Washington Expressway or Innerstate 495. Any empty highway would do, there he could really do his thing.

Mike was a thrill seeker by nature, with no respect for the law. If he was lucky he might catch the attention a of highway patrol officer, then the fun would really begin. He loved engaging the police in high speed chases. Most times he would usually cross the Prince Georges County, Maryland state line and lose his pursuers there. But if things got too hectic, he'd take the police for a wild ride into Virginia.

"Damn, Joe where the fuck is all the Feds at? Sleep?" He asked frustrated. "Ain't dis da nation's capitol? Where da fuck is all da bama ass police? Huh? These jokers never around when you need them? Huh?"

In his passenger seat sat Tonya Tompkins, aka T.T... By any measure, she was a dime piece. She was blessed with a beautiful golden brown complexion, with big bubbly light brown eyes and full succulent lips. Standing at an average 5'5", T.T.'s body was anything but. She was armed with a perfectly shaped heart behind and a pair of firm melon sized breasts. She had a body to die for. Other women envied it, while every hustler wanted to have her for his own.

Though they had only been dealing with each other for a short time, around a year, she had practically grown accustomed to her boyfriend's need for speed. Nevertheless, she didn't like it. Sometimes his speeding even scared her.

"Youngin' you done lost ya god damn mind? Or sumthin?" Tonya barked. "

Mike, you need ta slow da hell down..... Before we end up in D.C jail or worse.... on da morning news.... I swear you be lunchin' hard sometimes Joe!.... Like you been smokin' dat love boat!... Or a sherm stick..."

"Shawty, I got this!.... Calm ya nerves...... You know I can drive.... Has anything ever happened before? Huh?.... No!" He snapped.

"That's why they call 'em accidents Mike! It can happen to anyone at anytime!... Even da best of drivers!" She angrily exclaimed. "When I die I want it to be fa a reason.... Not cause my man has a led foot...... cause he was a speed demon!.... And would'nt slow da hell down..."

"Here you go wit dat shit again! You sound like a

damn broken record..." Mike said. "Shawty, don't go there wit dat.... T.T. you really know how to kill my joy. Fa real youngin'..... I hate when you talk like dat!... Stop talkin' 'bout dat death shit.... Ain't you ever heard death is in the tongue... It's in the bible..... Keep talkin' bout death and you gonna bring it on us....."

Immediately, Mike began to comply with her wishes, downshifting, smoothly breaking the car down to a reasonable speed. As he did so, he glared over at his girlfriend, as if to say 'I hope you happy now!'

"....Anyway, I'm hungry!... Let's go get somethin' ta eat...."

"Alright!" Mike agreed. "The only thing open this time of night is I-Hop!"

"....Dat's fine!" T.T. expressed.

Even in the dimly lit interior of the car, Mike's facial features stood out to T.T. The mean mug that was currently paced to his face, made the situation even worse. She had to admit, he was one ugly joker. But she loved him still. Sometimes she even wondered what she saw in him. Regardless, T.T was crazy about him. She worshipped the ground he walked on and vice versa.

"Mike I'm hungry! Let's go get somthin' ta eat!" T.T. suggested. Still fuming Mike was slow to answer his girlfriend. When he spoke it was clear he had an attitude.

"Whut you wanna eat?" Mike spat. "It's gettin' late!..... Can't you wait till we get home?"

"No!" T.T. whined. "I don't feel like cookin'... I'm hungry now!...."

T.T. looked at Mike with a pair of puppy dog eyes. He tried desperately to stand his ground, to stay mad at her, but he couldn't. He broke out into a wide tooth smile. Mike was putty in her hands, and he knew. Suffering from a somewhat low self esteem Mike felt lucky, even privileged to have her.

He knew she could have her pick of guys but T.T chose him.

Despite his physical appearance, as ugly as he was, T.T. never heard anyone say so. Not even in a joking manner. Mike was no joke; one couldn't disrespect him in any manner and not expect something to happen. The way he carried himself, he demanded respect. He had come up hard on the streets of Southeast D.C. and he was going hard every day, he was dirt poor with nothing to lose. Everyday he was out to prove it.

They say beauty is only skin deep, what Mike lacked physically he more than made up in the personality department. He had something called inner beauty. He was kind-hearted, caring and gentle to those who were close to him. Mike's inner being made him extremely attractive.

From day one, when they met, she saw past his physical limitations. He had one quality that she found very attractive, he was very confident. Mike stepped to her at a local Go-Go Club, when other guys were too intimidated by her beauty, to holler at her. In her book he got props for that alone.

T.T. chose not to judge him by his looks. Besides she had dealt with enough pretty boys to know they don't treat women right. They have too many options, too many temptations to do wrong. Armed with that fact, she decided to take the road less traveled. She began to date Mike, regardless of what anybody thought or said.

From the outside looking in, it appeared that T.T. and Mike were an odd couple. But appearances can be very misleading; they both shared the similar backgrounds. They were both street bred. T.T. was from a broken home. Her mother had her at a young age, so their relationship was more like sisters than mother/daughter. As a result T.T. grew up fast and came and went as she pleased. She became exposed to adult situations at an early age. She became streetwise, grown before her time. Still in many ways T.T. was very much child like. She was a pretender, a wishful thinker. She fancied a future with Mike, with all the trimming, a car, kids, a house and a white picketfence. She thought eventually she could change him, save him. T.T. thought she could get Mike out the game. But it was all just a dream. In all reality it wasn't to be. Mike was going to do what he did till someone decided to end his life. Mike on the other hand lived in reality, he was a realist. Things were the way they were, not the way he wanted them to be.

Mike was a risk taker by nature, constantly taking unnecessary chances with his life. As a professional stick up kid, death was always in the back of his mind. He always knew, his next breathe could be his last. He readily accepted that fact from the first moment he put a gun in his hand. Death befalls almost every stick-up kid; it's just a matter of time. Stick-up kids didn't retire, there were no 401k's in this line of work. The only retirement plan was a bullet in the head. Mike knew too, still he hated to be reminded of it.

Mike knew the law of the land, 'what comes around goes around'. One day he would be on the wrong end of a gun, staring down the barrel, waiting and wondering if it was his time to go. Mike Jones lived for the moment. He lived everyday as if it were his last. He readily accepted his fate whatever it maybe.

At the tender age of seventeen, physically Mike was man amongst boys, a man-child. He stood at six feet tall, extremely well built, short wavy hair, jet black complexion and suspiciously slanted eyes. His nose was so big that looked out of place on his face. He was also armed with a pair of gigantic, scarred up hands, from countless street fights.

On the streets of Southeast, D.C. Mike was known as a knockout artist. In the hood they called him 'Iron Mike' or 'Baby Tyson'. He was blessed with a raw inner strength, brute power that one just couldn't acquire from exercise. At an early age Mike got involved in boxing. He was attracted to the brutality of the sport. Almost immediately trainers saw his untapped potential. They thought if it was proper channeled and with a lot of hardwork he could eventually become a title contender or even a champion, in the future.

But like so many others before him though, Mike would ultimately fall victim to the ever-present allure of the streets. Mike was short-sighted and more importantly, poor. His future was now, so he took to the drug game out of necessity. He had to eat, it was that simple.

A product of a broken home, Mike was an only child; he never knew his father. From birth he had a hard knock life. His mother couldn't adequately provide for him, nor could she control him. So she placed him in a group home at a young age. In the system he bounced around for a couple of years, until he ran away. Thinking he was old enough to take care of himself.

At a young age, Mike embarked on a life of crime, which eventually got him arrested for grand theft auto. This crime landed him in the juvenile correctional system. He was sent to Oak Hill juvenile facility for a short stint. During that time he learned the tricks of the trade.

Upon his release Mike dabbled in selling rock, but he quickly realized that it wasn't for him. He felt like a sitting target. He was always either ducking the police or the stick-up boys. He grew tired of this cat and mouse game.

One day after getting robbed by the stick-up boys, Mike went and got a gun and robbed someone else, from a nearby neighborhood. And from that day on, he became a stick-up kid. Mike figured once they made money he would come along and take it. He grew to be just as deadly with a gun as he was with his fists. Even at a young age, he was quickly becoming one of D.C.'s most notorious stick-up kids.

If you had it Mike was coming to get it. His reputation was growing daily.

****

Hogtied to a chair, Jerry could barely see through his bloodied and almost swollen shut eyelids. Still he saw the menacing dark skin figure as clear as day. His robber's face and physical description burned in his mind's eye. This was a face he wouldn't soon forget if ever. If he ever got out of this, he swore to himself, he would make his assailant pay, with their life.

On the street it was a well known fact that, Jerry was one of the biggest drug dealers in D.C. His activities had come to Mike Jones' attention. Mike had watched Jerry for about two weeks, following him home, before he felt comfortable with his daily routine, to rob him.

Now currently, he was a prisoner in his own home, the victim of a home invasion. He was in the process of being robbed. Mike had ransacked his home, in a desperate attempt to find his money and narcotic stash.

Now Mike was resulting to torture to get the necessary information about the whereabouts of Jerry's secret stash location. Though it was unnecessary, Mike spit on the hot iron for emphasis and watched as his saliva quickly evaporated. He then yanked the cord out the wall, gripping the hot iron; he walked slowly towards his victim.

Jerry's eyes grew wide with fear, as he watched his captor slowly approach. Suddenly, he began to have second thoughts about withholding that information, he started to blurt out the location of his stash, hidden within the house. He even began to question his own involvement in the drug game. Right now he wanted no parts of what was about to happen to him. It wasn't worth his life.

"Youngin' dis ya last chance..... Now, where da fuck iz dat dough at?.... Nigger, I know it in here?.... Somewhere?... Where is it?...." Mike spat, waving the iron inches from his face. In fact it was so close he could feel the intense heat it emitted.

Though Jerry was completely terrified at this point, somehow he managed to hold his ground and not tell the whereabouts of his stash.

With a sinister grin on his face, Mike stared his victim down. As if to give him on last chance to speak before he began to torture him.

"Youngin', you goin' hard huh?" Mike barked. "You tryin' ta carry me like I'm some motherfuckin' bama huh?.... Alright, youngin' you asked for it...... Hold dis!...."

In a blink of an eye, Mike struck. He raised the hot iron and pressed it down hard on his face. Jerry tried his best to avoid the iron, by wiggling in his chair. It was to no avail, the iron easily found his mark.

"AAAAAAAAAAAAAAAwwwwwwwwww!" Jerry screamed.

The repulsing smell of burning human flesh hung thick in the air. Quietly, the scent almost made Mike want to vomit. But he managed to suppress the strong urge to do so. Instead, he stepped away from his victim and admired his handiwork. All he saw was blood, raw flesh and the outline of an iron on the side of Jerry's face.

Tears streamed down Jerry's cheeks. This unusual form of torture had bought the bitch out of him. There was no way he could withstand another strike from a hot iron.

Suddenly, through a sock that was stuffed halfway down his throat, Jerry began to utter something. The sound wasn't understandable. But Mike knew the language of pain, it was unmistakable. He had broken Jerry and he knew it.

"Look, in da kitchen!.... Jerry mumbled. "It's in da coca cola cans...."

Mike moved with the quickness, rushing out the back bedroom into the kitchen. There on the counter he spotted what he was looking for, a six pack of coca cola. He picked up the six pack and shook it. For all intents and purposes it looked like and felt like a real six pack of soda. Thinking he'd come up empty, Mike flew into a violent rage. He thought that Jerry was trying to play him. With the six pack of soda in one hand and his gun in the other he walked back towards the room. He was through playing with Jerry, if he didn't tell now he was a dead man.

"Youngin' I'ma blow ya fuckin' brains out Joe!...." He barked. "....I'm tireda playin' wit you!...."

Fear seized Jerry, his eyes grew to the size of half dollars. He began to rock back and forth in his chair, shaking his head. No, No his body language seemed to beg.

"Look inside the cans!..." Jerry pled. "...They fake pop cans.... Twist off da tops.... da dope inside!... five ounces of raw dope!..."

Hearing the desperation in his voice, Mike stopped in his tracks. This time he followed Jerry's instructions to the tee. Just like Jerry had promised, the drugs magically appeared, five ounces of raw heroin began to drop into his hands. This wasn't the payday he was looking for, but it beat a blank. He could easily sell this product to dope boys around his way. For a fraction of it's cost of course. He was just trying to get rid of it though.

Mike kicked himself for not being down with this hiding place. He wondered how many other drug stashes had avoided his detection, during robberies. Mike didn't know who thought this shit up but it was clever as hell. It looked and felt like the actual product. Money buys loyalty in the hood.

Now that Mike had the stash he knew it was time to finish the job. He had to kill Jerry. He couldn't let a powerful drug lord like Jerry live. Jerry had too much money. He knew money bought allies; money brings death in the ghetto. When placed in the proper hands. Mike wasn't so much worried about Jerry himself; no he wouldn't do the killing. Guys like him were too concerned with their status in life, they didn't want to lose their money, women and cars. He was more concerned with the soldiers he would hire.

Murder was strictly business to Mike. As he took aim at Jerry's head, a sudden knock on the door stopped him from pulling the trigger. He hadn't expected anyone to come by. After all this was Jerry's house he lived alone.

Silently, Mike crept to the peep hole and took a look out. On the other side of the door he saw a young girl waiting patiently. She knocked repeatedly, determined to gain entrance. She appeared to be in her early teens. This was Jerry's little sister, Sharon. She had stopped by to collect the payment on a promise her brother made her for getting good grades on her report card. She had done her part now it was time that he did his. As promised he was going to give her some money to buy her the kind tennis shoes she wanted. She was going to buy a pair of new Air Jordan tennis shoes that just came out. Sharon had her heart set on it.

Mike's first thought was to wait her out. After watching silently for twenty minutes, it appeared she wasn't budging from the door. Dumbfounded, he didn't know what to do next. He reluctantly decided to abandon his idea of killing Jerry. Though Mike was a stone cold killer, he wasn't down for killing innocent kids. Today was Jerry's lucky day.

Silently, Mike made his way out the backdoor of the townhouse. He cursed his dumb luck in many ways he hoped this day wouldn't come back to haunt him.

****

The International House of Pancakes was jammed packed, as usual after a Go-Go show. Mike and T.T. had stopped in to get a bite to eat. They were more than a little hungry. Besides they knew that they'd better eat now, because tomorrow they'd be sleeping in late.

****

Two men sat inside a car in the International House of Pancakes parking lot, a drug lord had just finished making a transaction, when a couple exiting the restaurant caught one man's eye. At first he was drawn to the sexy shape of the female, but it was the male who really caught his attention. The dude's face looked real familiar for some unknown reason. Jerry swore like hell he knew the guy. He wondered from what and where?

It had been almost six months since he had been robbed and beaten. When a person experiences a traumatic incident like that they don't soon forget, no matter how much time has gone by. Every moment of the day, you live with it, especially, if you take a loss and if you're living the street life. You live with it until you can get even. You can't ever forget about it no matter how bad you may want to. Jerry remembered his incident vividly.

"I Don't know where I know dat bama from?..... But his face looks real familiar youngin'?'..... Gary I swear I know dat Bama"!..." Jerry stated.

"From where?" His enforcer asked. "You usta serve youngin' or something? Maybe he was a customer?...."

Sitting in his car in deep thought, Jerry continued to ponder hard the situation. Then suddenly a light went off in his head. His memory came rushing back. Jerry's facial expression suddenly changed, a mean mug instantly appeared.

"I got it Joe!" He snapped. "Dat's da Bama who robbed me! I'm tellin' you!.... Dat's him!... I'll never ever forget dat face...."

"You sure?" The enforcer questioned. "You positive?... I'll jump out and do him right now...."

"Na, Joe not right here! Too many witnesses...." Jerry exclaimed. Plus da police right inside dat joint!...."

"Well, what you wanna do?" The enforcer asked.

"Follow him!" Jerry remarked. "First chance we get we kill'em!"

"What about da broad?" He questioned. "Fuck it!... Kill her too!"

Stopping at the International House of Pancakes turned out to be a costly mistake. Mike had robbed so many hustlers he could barely remember exactly who he had robbed. Yet they never forgot him. It wasn't good for a dude like him to be out in public. Mike was either fearless or just plain stupid. Being at simply at the wrong place at the wrong time, was about to cost Mike Jones dearly.

The meal seemed to have hit the spot. T.T. and Mike didn't make another complaint about hunger. Another thing the meal achieved was dulling Mike's senses. Now he was quite sleepy. He appeared a bit sluggish in his movements and his reactions.

Mike downshifted his Nissan 300zx, slowing for a red light at an upcoming intersection. When he reached the intersection, he did something he normally did when he was tired. He reached down and pulled up the emergency brake. This rendered the car motionless. Getting in to bed dominated his thoughts. Preoccupied with that notion, he threw caution to the wind. He never noticed the black BMW 745i sedan following him.

Mike pulled smoothly to the stop light, never once did he check his surroundings. The car immediately right behind he went unnoticed. Without warning, the BMW inched forward, closer to its intended target. The would-be assassins crept ever so close to Mike's vehicle. Their timing was impeccable, they caught the changing of the stop light and they made their move. Oblivious to what was happening, Mike continued to make small talk with T.T.

"...Dat omelet was good as shit!" Mike remarked. "Some kinda wonderful!...." T.T. replied, "....How many times you gonna say dat Joe?.... I know! If you say dat one mo' time.... I'll be no mo' good..."

"Stop hatin' shawty!" Mike joked. "Give credit, where credit is due!"

".....Whatever!" T.T. shot back.

Mike loved the fact that his girlfriend had a sense of humor. It made them even closer. He knew he could talk to her about anything. Because she was who she was, it made it that much easier for him to be himself. She was his backbone. He leaned on her for moral support. When things got crazy on the streets, Mike knew he could come home and be at peace. No matter how many dudes he robbed or killed, at home he was just Mike.

Glazing into her eyes for a moment he was lost in thought. He thought how fortunate he was to have her in his corner. Momentarily he was distracted.

The BMW pulled alongside Mike's car, and the back window rolled down quickly. A black Tec-nine was suddenly produced from the car window. Gary squeezed the hairpin trigger, spraying the car with a barrage of bullets. He kept firing until the clip was empty.

From a distance the shooting sounded like the Fourth of July. Non-stop, bullet after bullet after bullet found its mark. The bullets ripped through the car so badly, it began to resemble Swiss cheese. The thin sheet metal was no match for the weapon.

The couple didn't stand a chance. They were riddled with countless bullets in the face and upper torso. Literally the car was blood soaked.

Jerry paused momentarily, peering into the car. What he saw pleased him, it bought a sinister smile to his face. The bullet riddled body of his enemy lay motionless. Gary had extracted the ultimate measure of revenge for him. Jerry was immune to the fact that another innocent life was loss in the process.

Quickly, Jerry mashed his foot on the gas, sending the car lurching forward. The assassins sped into the night, managing to flee the crime scene before the police arrived.

Ironically, Mike was armed, but he never got a chance to even pull his pistol. Mike lay lifeless slumped over the wheel. Finally all the dirt he had done had caught up to him. He had lived by the gun and sadly he died by the gun. The violent ghetto life cycle had come full circle.

Game Over

Shannon Holmes is the Essence Magazine Best Seller Author, of B-More Careful, Badgirlz, and Never Go Home Again. Shannon is currently working on his next novel "Every Thing Ain't fa Everybody."

The KISS

| Natasha Philips

Nayla laid there thinking what had she gotten herself into. She rolled over to see Lena lying next to her sleeping. Nayla couldn't help but think how beautiful Lena was. Her skin was like smooth caramel, her eyes, the perfect shape, and her body was so soft. Nayla reached out and touched Lena's face. She made sounds that made Nayla's stomach ache.

Nayla got up out of bed and headed for the shower. She did not know how things got so complicated. It all started at Jai's graduation party, two days ago. Jai dated Lena for six months when we were juniors. Lena broke it off, because Jai cheated on her with a woman who was old enough to be his mother. Nayla met up with Paige and Hope at Luigi Pizzeria on 8th Street. They planned on being late to the party, so things would be really popping when they got there.

After walking ten minutes from the pizzeria they

arrived at Jai's house. It was set back from the street, and there was a large tree in the yard. People were sitting on the steps to the porch and the front door was wide open. They could hear the music blasting as they approached the crowd. Nayla instantly lost Paige and Hope when they entered the house. She was sure they had made their way into the room where everyone was dancing. Hope was the squad leader of their school's Step Troop. She loved to dance and show off in front of others. Paige was trying to kick it to this junior, who she thought was from a rich family. She was a gold digger and had no shame about it. Nayla didn't socialize with most of the kids in her school. She preferred to spend her time with staff at school. She usually gossiped with teachers and other staff of Humboldt High. Nayla knew so much gossip that teachers would trade bits of information with her. At the party all she wanted to do was discover who was there and what they were doing.

There had to be at least a hundred bodies at the party. Even the backyard was crowded. She knew most of them from graduation rehearsals. Nayla couldn't even see who was sitting in chairs, as she made her way through the herd of people. She didn't like crowds so she ventured up the short staircase. She walked into one room and saw six guys she didn't know smoking a blunt and watching the movie Half Baked. Nayla couldn't help herself so she opened the next door and was sorry that she did. There were five kids who she had randomly seen in school. They were all naked and all Nayla saw was a heap of tits and ass. She heard the moans and felt paralyzed, as she watched the group pleasure each other. One of the guys caught her staring into the room and asked her if she wanted to join in. Nayla heard herself say no, but couldn't take her eyes off of what was happening in that room. Someone squeezed passed her in the tiny hallway and walked into the room. He was naked in two seconds and was rubbing his dick while he watched these two girls eat each other out. Nayla had only seen such things in porno movies. This was definitely better than any of the movies she had seen. After being engrossed in the orgy room for five minutes, Nayla tried to open the other door, which she thought was the bathroom, but it was locked. She thought, "at least they were smart enough to lock the door."

She worked her way back down the stairs, and walked back through the crowd and noticed that there was a door off the side of the kitchen. Nayla was wondering were Jai was, because she hadn't seen him since she arrived at the party. She made her way to the door and slowly began to walk down the stairs. She heard Jai laughing and walked into the room to see Hope being licked down her neck almost to her breast, by Bryant, one of the boys on the school's basketball team. Everyone was laughing and screaming. When Jai saw Nayla he got up and said, "What up, you want to play." Nayla asked, "What are you playing." "Truth or Dare," Jai replied. Nayla had heard of the game but was not quite sure what it was, so she asked Jai to explain it. Jai told her that if you are selected then you get to pick either a truth or a dare. If you pick truth the person who selected you will get to ask you any question they want to, and if you pick a dare they can ask you to do something. He said the only rule was that you couldn't ask a person to have any type of sex, and that included oral. Nayla thought this sounded a little risky, but why not. She liked the players, so things might get interesting.

She joined the game of Truth or Dare and watched this girl named Kisha get felt up by Jai. Kisha was currently dating Jai. She was a quiet girl, who was also known for giving head in many locations around school. Nayla wondered if Jai knew this about her. Bryant chose Lena who selected dare. They should have just called it the game of dare, because no one seemed to ever select truth. Bryant dared Lena to kiss Nayla while he counted to ten. Nayla was shocked that Lena was even considering doing it. Lena was popular in school and all the boys thought she was hot. She seemed so straight; so when she got on her knees and crawled over to where Nayla was sitting, she felt her stomach go warm.

Lena crawled right up to and in between Nayla's legs and slowly began to kiss her. Nayla instantly felt her panties get wet as Lena slipped her tongue into her mouth. She had never remembered feeling so aroused; even with the six boyfriends she had been through in her four years of high-school. She wondered what Lena was thinking. It seemed that she liked what was happening. Nayla put her hands in Lena's hair and Lena wrapped her arms around the small of Nayla's back. When Lena heard Bryant say ten, she didn't pull away so fast. Actually, she pulled away slowly. Nayla didn't hear anything while Lena was kissing her, but after-wards Jai said, "Damn y'all made that look so fucking good." Everyone else was kind of quiet. Lena said, "It's my turn." She picked Jai and he selected dare. Lena dared him to kiss Bryant. Jai said "hell no I ain't no homo." Lena said, "I did-n't say that when I was asked to kiss Nayla." "Well I'm not doing it." Lena got up and left the room. She was not going to play if the rules weren't the same for everyone." At this point it seemed like the game was over, because Hope left and so did Bryant. Nayla got up and left the room. She had always known that she was attracted to girls. She remem-bered once when she was in the girl's locker room, she couldn't help but look at Lanisa's body and feel like she wanted to touch her breasts. Lanisa was a cheerleader for the basketball team, who was famous for her splits.

That kiss really messed up Nayla's head. She kept replaying the moment over and over again. Nayla felt like she was starting to panic. She had tried her whole life to stay away from these feelings, because she knew that if something like this would ever happen, there would be no turning back. Nayla left the party alone. She needed to be by herself. Nayla felt her eyes fill with tears, because she knew that from this moment on her life would be forever changed. She went to Jai's party knowing herself in one way and leaving not wondering, but knowing that she was a lesbian. Nayla closed her eyes and she could feel Lena's lips again. She remembered the softness of them and the sweetness of her breath against her top lip. Nayla couldn't help but get moist between her legs. There was no more fighting. She could feel her body relax with resolution.

Nayla was about to jump into the shower, when she caught a glimpse of herself in the mirror. She had three large hickies on her neck and was wondering how she was going to cover it up. Nayla knew that if her mother saw them it she would beat her ass, if she knew that another girl gave them to her. Nayla knew that she had to go to Church tomorrow and teach Bible study. She thought about her family and how they would handle the news about her being gay, if she ever told them. She knew that she would never be disowned, but feared that she would be talked about and treated differently. She knew her family would not know how to act around her, so situations would always be uncomfortable. As the water beat over Nayla's body, she began to replay the last six hours.

The day after Jai's party she went to school with Lena on her mind. Nayla knew that she would see Lena in her fourth period English class. She didn't know how to act in front of Lena. They had never been close friends, but always exchanged hellos. When fourth period came Nayla felt the palms of her hands getting sweaty. She also felt excited about seeing Lena again, but couldn't believe how nervous she was. Nayla was never a person who felt intimidated by others, but she was definitely afraid of herself and Lena. Mr. Elliot came in and Nayla began to relax thinking that Lena did not show up to school. Just when she began to relax and the class quieted down, Lena walked in. At first Nayla kept her head down afraid to look at her, but before she even lifted her head Lena walked passed her desk and dropped a note. Luckily, Lena sat two rows behind her. Nayla didn't read the note until class was almost over. It simply said "Meet me at Randall Park after school. We need to talk." Nayla turned around and looked at Lena, who was staring back into her eyes, but she couldn't read the expression on her face.

It was the longest day of Nayla's life. She waited for two-thirty to arrive, as if her life depended on it, she couldn't think. What would she say to Lena and what would Lena say or do to her? Nayla walked into the park and sat on one of the benches facing a jungle gym. The day was warm and the air moist with anticipation. As she watched the kids play she looked at her ten-dollar watch and wondered what was taking Lena so long. She thought about leaving, but decided to wait ten more minutes. It was already five minutes to three.

Ten minutes later when Nayla began to walk out of the park, she saw Lena walking toward her. Nayla didn't know what to think or how to feel. For a moment she thought that she should start running the other way. Lena walked right up to her and said, "Come with me." There were no other words spoken between them. They walked for fifteen minutes up Grand Street. Lena turned and walked up a path to a large gray house with white shutters. She took out her key and unlocked the door. Nayla didn't know what was waiting for her on the other side of this door. They walked in. Lena closed the door. Nayla was too busy looking at the large spiral staircase to notice that Lena began to take off her clothes, behind her. Nayla turned around and saw Lena, completely nude. Lena walked up to Nayla, looked into her eyes and began to slowly take off Nayla's jacket, then her shirt, bra, pants, and panties. They stood facing each other. They were so close that Nayla could smell the scent of her body. Nayla felt the warmth between her legs. She couldn't help what was happening to her body. She really didn't know Lena, but she knew that she wanted to taste her and feel her body on top of hers. Nayla's body was fabulous. Her cocoa skin, shapely hips, and neatly braided cornrows, drove Lena to a place that she never thought she would visit.

In the front hall of her house, Lena reached out and ran her hands over Nayla's breast. She felt Nayla's nipples harden under her touch. Nayla moved forward until she felt Lena against her and instantly the hairs on her body stood on end. She moved to Nayla's lips and then down her neck. Nayla rubbed the palms of her hands down the center of Lena's back until she could hold her ass in them. She slid to her knees tasting all, and savoring Lena's nipples on the way down. Nayla ran her tongue on the insides of Lena's thighs. She could feel Lena's body quiver with desire. Nayla put Lena's leg over her shoulder and tasted her. Lena began to moan and gyrate her hips over Nayla's mouth. Nayla could feel Lena's cum in her mouth. She swallowed, moved her tongue over and around her clit, until her lips completely sur-rounded it. Nayla sucked and Lena opened her mouth with noises of pleasure. Nayla felt her juices run down the inside of her thighs. She had already reached her height without even being touched. She laid Lena down on top of their clothes and inserted her pointer and middle fingers together inside of her. Nayla heard Lena grunt and saw her bite her top lip. She kept her fingers moving inside and tasted her. At one point Lena pushed herself up on her elbow, so she could look at Nayla. She smiled and began to ride on Nayla's fingers. By the time she reached orgasm, Lena was leaning up against the bottom of the staircase.

Once Nayla heard Lena climax, she kissed her way back to her lips. Lena then forcefully put Nayla on her back and tied her to the railing with her sock. She could feel Lena's tongue trace her hips and under the crease of her breast. Lena could feel Nayla's body tense up under hers and was aroused by the grunts that she was making. Before Nayla knew it Lena had her head between her legs and was savoring her clit. Nayla easily undid her tied hands and leaned up to pull Lena's body over hers; until her pussy was over Nayla's face. Lena bent over licking the inside of Nayla's thighs, the crease of her hips and then back to the spot. They both pleasured each other until they felt their bodies shiver with ecstasy. Nayla and Lena fell over panting with smiles on their faces.

They lay in their sweat and easily rubbing the tips of their fingers over each other's body. When Lena heard a noise in the garage. She jumped up and grabbed Nayla's hand. They grabbed their clothes in their arms and ran up the spiral staircase. Lena locked the door to her room and said to Nayla, "Don't worry. My father never comes to my room when he gets off work. He usually stays home for about an hour and then he leaves to see his girlfriend. My mother died two years ago from Cancer." Nayla said, "I'm sorry to hear that." They sat on the edge of Lena's canopy bed and listened to her father's footsteps downstairs. Lena pulled Nayla down onto the bed. She moved her body close to Nayla and said, "What are we doing?" Nayla lay there thinking about what had just happened and wondering what Lena was feeling. She hadn't even had a conversation with her and really had no clue who she was and what she wanted. Nayla heard Lena's light snores and the door slam beneath them, only then could she drift off to sleep.

Nayla got out of the shower. It had to be at least ten o'clock at night and she was shocked that her cell phone didn't have a message from her mother. She usually called her mother when she was going out after school, but today Nayla was a little busy. She walked back into Lena's bedroom and put on her clothes that were all wrinkled from the days events. Lena sat up in the bed and said in a whisper, "I'm not sure how I feel about today. Don't get me wrong, it was great and I loved being with you. But I don't know where we are going from here or what I want from you. We don't even know each other, but when I kissed you at Jai's party, I felt something I didn't expect to feel. I really don't know how to explain it." Nayla said, "I feel the same way. When you touch me it makes me feel alive, not just my body, but my soul. All I want to know is where we go from here?" Lena stared blankly at her and said, "I don't know. Maybe we should slow down and try to figure this out. We're just going for the ride and are not quite sure where we are going to end up." Nayla said, "Is that a bad thing. Do you regret us fucking? Just be real with me." "I don't know. I'm just going to take it easy," Lena said. "What does that mean Lena?" Nayla's voice was getting loud. She felt herself getting angry, but wasn't quite sure why. Lena looked at her and said, "Don't be angry Nayla, just give me a chance to figure all of this out." Nayla picked up her book bag and left Lena's room. Lena could hear the door slam down stairs.

Nayla started walking toward her house, but when she looked up she didn't know where she was. She just kept thinking, why? It was Lena who started the whole thing. She kissed her at Jai's party, she dropped the note and asked her to meet her at the park, she had invited me back to her house, and she was the first to get naked. Nayla heard her cell phone ring and knew she was about to hear her mother's mouth. It was fifteen minutes to midnight. "Nayla, where are you?"

"Mom, I have a test tomorrow, so I went to study with Paige and Hope." "It's almost midnight and I want you home now." Nayla hung up the phone and quickly figured out that she was only a couple of blocks away from home. She walked those three blocks, thinking of Lena and feeling hurt. Nayla was upset with herself, for letting Lena in. She was the kind of person that never let anyone close enough to hurt her, including her best friends Paige and Hope. They were her girls, but she dare not share every thought, especially because Nayla knew Paige had a big mouth. She could never keep a secret. Once Nayla tested her and she told. She met them at freshman orientation. Nayla remembered Paige being the loudest one in the auditorium, when they were getting their first program. Paige and Hope had known each other since sixth grade and had purposely chosen the same high school, because they were afraid of being jumped, because they were freshmen. They had heard plenty of stories about the first day in high school and decided that it wasn't worth the chance; at least they had each other.

Nayla walked up to her front door. Dreading the lecture she was about to get from her mother. Nayla had never really trusted her mother. Rhonda had Nayla when she was sixteen and wasn't around much when she was a kid. Nayla was raised by her maternal grandparents until she was eleven. Nayla only went to live with her mother when she was thirteen, because she got married. Nayla's grandfather was extremely religious and wouldn't let her live with her mother while she was living with a man who was not her husband. So Rhonda married this guy that she wasn't in love with just to have Nayla come live with her. She admitted to Nayla that she only married him, so she could have her. This didn't make Nayla feel better; it only made her feel guilty. She knew that her mother had given up a chance for real happiness, because Rhonda was torn between the church and her love for men. When Rhonda was eleven and got her period for the first time, she was told that she could only were skirts from now on, by her father. He ruled his home with an iron fist and no one dared to openly challenge him. It was expected that everyone attend church at least three times a week. He set the rules and no one questioned them. According to this sect of the Pentecostal Religion, once you are married there is no such thing as divorce. The only way someone could get re-married was if their spouse died, so when she married Nayla's stepfather, she gave up her chances of marrying someone whom she really loved.

Nayla walked into her home and immediately heard her mother belt her name from the living room. She looked at Nayla in a suspicious way and said, "Where were you really? You know I had plenty of study dates too when I was your age. Come here." Nayla walked over and said, "I was really with Paige and Hope. We have a biology test tomorrow." Nayla forgot to zip her fleece up over her neck. Rhonda looked at her neck, pointed and said, "So, where did those come from?" Nayla stumbled over her words and said, "mom I'm seventeen don't you think I'm old enough to have a boyfriend." Nayla knew she had to lie, because her mother had grown up way too religious to understand her being a lesbian. Rhonda then said, "Don't get smart, I know you are old enough to have a boyfriend. Why didn't you tell me you had a boyfriend?"

"I don't know. It feels strange to talk to your mother about these things."

"Well Nayla, you know you can tell me anything."

"Yeah mom, I know. I'm going to bed. Goodnight." Nayla was happy that her mom didn't go off on a tangent about why she had lied to her. Nayla walked upstairs to her bedroom. Her room was lavender and simply decorated with a bed, stereo, television and two dressers. She had a big poster of Queen Latifah over her bed that she loved more than anything. Nayla was into old school rap. She took off her clothes and lay in her bed thinking of Lena and being afraid of what would happen next.

Nayla woke up late for school. She was thinking about staying home, but she didn't want Lena to think she was avoiding her, so she went. When she arrived at school everyone was already in their first period class. Nayla had to wait for a pass to her class at the attendance office, because she was late to school. As she walked toward her first period chemistry class Nayla saw Paige walking into the girls' bathroom. Nayla followed her into the bathroom. Paige heard a person walk into the bathroom behind her, so she turned around to face Nayla. "Girl what happened to you yesterday afternoon? Hope and I were looking all over for you."

"I had to go take care of something for my mother."

"Nayla, you don't look so well. Are you alright?"

"I'm fine, just a little tired." Nayla hoped that she wouldn't run into   Lena today, but she knew that it was impossible, because they had the same fourth period class. "Paige was too busy looking at herself in the mirror to pay anymore attention to Nayla. "I'll see you at lunch Paige-bye."

"See you later." Nayla walked into her chemistry class and by this time she had already missed more than half the class. Nayla couldn't hear anything Ms. Tumin was saying, because she was too preoccupied with what was going to happen when she saw Lena.

When chemistry class was over Nayla was making her way to the locker room to get ready for gym, when she saw

Lena. Nayla couldn't believe what she saw. She felt like she wanted to throw up. Lena was up against the lockers with this guy that Nayla didn't even know. While this guy was kissing her on her neck, Lena looked over his shoulder to see Nayla staring in her eyes. Nayla hadn't even noticed that she stopped to look. As soon as Lena made eye contact with Nayla, she walked away. Nayla could feel her eyes fill with tears, but she refused to shed one. She walked into the locker room and realized that she was late, because all the other girls had finished changing and were making their way into the gym. Nayla had begun to change her clothes when she felt somebody take hold of her wrist. "Nayla don't be mad." Nayla looked at Lena and felt speechless. "I don't want to hurt you, but I'm trying to figure things out for myself." They stood face to face and Nayla couldn't help the tears that fell to her cheeks. "You don't want to hurt me? You made love to me yesterday Lena, and I walk into school to see some guy all over your neck.

What the hell are you talking about?"

"I care about you, but I don't know if I can be in a relationship with a girl."

"Well you should have thought about that before you fucked me." Lena moved close to Nayla.

Lena saw how hurt she was and it bothered her. "Nayla, what happened between us is special and I've never felt this way about another girl, I'm scared." Lena leaned in and gently kissed Nayla. She pushed Lena against the lockers and looked into her eyes. Lena's eyes began to water. Nayla picked her up off the floor and held her so she could feel her body against hers. She felt the warm inside of Lena's mouth and slipped her hands under the back of her shirt undoing her bra. Nayla walked holding Lena into the back shower stalls, which no one ever used. She peeled off Lena's shirt and cupped her breast in her hand. Nayla slipped her hands down Lena's pants and felt that she was already wet, so she put her fingers inside her. Lena's moans were getting louder, so Nayla put her other hand over her mouth. Lena began to lick the inside of her hand and sucking her fingers. Nayla could feel her pussy throbbing. She wanted Lena and she wanted Lena to want her. Nayla looked at Lena in the height of her excitement and said, "I'm going to make sure that you never want anyone else." Nayla had never felt like this and was surprised that she had been so honest with Lena. Just as Lena climaxed, Nayla looked up toward the opening to the showers and almost screamed when she saw Hope and Paige watching them.

Nayla moved her body as to get a better look at Hope and Paige. Lena looked around Nayla, grabbed her bra and shirt. And then took off out of the showers into the bathroom at the other end of the locker room. Paige and Hope did not say a word. They had stumbled upon Lena and Nayla, because they were looking for a place to ditch third period history class. Nayla noticed that she was on the floor when she heard the girls re-enter the locker room from the gym. Nayla got up and walked pass them without saying anything.

Paige and Hope could not believe their eyes and had no idea that Nayla liked girls. "What are we going to say to Nayla, Paige?"

"I don't know. Did you know that something was going on between Nayla and Lena?"

"No I had no idea." As soon as Hope finished saying those words, she remembered the kiss at Jai's party. "Paige at Jai's party Lena kissed Nayla in a Truth or Dare game and it was a good one too."

"Obviously it was good, because they were completely wrapped. I can't believe that it took them almost five minutes to notice that we were watching them."

"Well we're going to go look for Nayla as soon as this period is over."

Paige and Hope looked all over the building. They went to Nayla's fourth period class, but she wasn't there. Lena was also in that class, but she wasn't there either. Paige began to get nervous. She soon realized that neither Nayla nor Lena were still in the building. They decided that they would leave school early, during their lunch period and go to Nayla's house. Nayla's mother worked so she could go home in the middle of the day and no one would ever be the wiser.

When Paige and Hope reached Nayla's house they heard Jay Z blasting through the open windows. Paige started banging on the front door and Hope was constantly ringing the doorbell. Nayla heard the door and the banging, but refused to acknowledge either. She sat on the floor in the living room writing some poetry and thinking about Lena. Nayla was so embarrassed and she knew that Paige would probably tell everyone, because she could never keep a secret. Nayla didn't know what happened to Lena after she fled the bathroom stall. Nayla went straight home. Eventually, Paige and Hope left after about ten minutes of banging and ringing. She knew that they would be back, so she decided to go out for a walk and she knew right where to go.

Nayla walked for about fifteen minutes until she found herself in front of Lena's door. She wanted to ring the bell or call her. Nayla didn't have her number. After pacing in front of Lena's house for ten minutes. Nayla finally got up the nerve to ring her doorbell. She rang the bell and considered running away, because of the nauseous feeling in her stomach but she couldn't move her feet. Nayla waited for a minute and was about to walk away when Lena opened the door, looking like she had the weight of the world on her shoulders. Nayla looked at her and quietly said, "What's your last name?"

Natasha currently resides in Las Vegas where she is hard at work on her next novel "A Woman's Touch." Natasha can be reached at Natasha@jacksonpress.net

In Search of Chucky Gee

| Joe Margolis

Charlie

In my short life I've learned one thing. Love makes people do crazy shit. As for me in the name of love, I became a white boy who'd do anything to be black. The name's Charlie, Charlie Goldberg from Durham, N.C. and It was the summer before my senior year in high school when this girl stole my heart. She just didn't know it. I was too scared to cross that line. I mean she was black and I didn't know what my parents would say. Plus she was two years older than me and in college, at North Carolina Central University, one of the biggest black colleges in the state.

At the time I was a bagger at a Food Fresh super-market. I didn't really need the money. My parents would've given me the world, but by the time I was 13 I was tired of depending on 'em. The money was there, but it was like the only time they paid me any real attention was when I'd mess up in school. Otherwise, I was left to fend for myself, which wasn't always pleasant. Nothing in my crazy world of being bullied and picked on in school seemed to mean much to them as long as I continued to make A's. I hated to see it like that, but it was what it was. So as soon as I was 15, meaning old enough to earn my own money, I claimed as much independence as I could by joining the rest of the teenaged working world. For the next two years it was all about the money for me, gas money, clothes money, hanging out money, money saved up for college. As for my academics, I still did my thing but it was all about earning a scholarship so I could leave Durham and never come back. Fuck pleasing my parents. You know?

But then along came Shalese and it became all about her. It was strange at first. I'd never let myself be attracted to a black girl before, but there was something about this girl that spelled F-I-N-E.

First off, she was confident. I could tell because she was sweet with everyone she came across. Most females I knew were too insecure to be like that. In conversation she made you feel like you were the most important in her world. Fellas, just imagine feeling understood and accepted by a girl like Shalese. So sexy and graceful, light-skinned about 5'3" with this cute school-girl face with raised check bones, chinky eyes and a beautiful smile which she never minded flashing. And that ass, fellas, was something to behold. I mean it defied all reason that such a small frame could be so curvy and hold such a soft-looking, round, voluptuous ass. Trust me when I say, she was a healthy young lady.

That's not what made her special though. A wise man once wrote a woman's worth is shown in her ability to influence a man's course. He must have been right because Shalese's worth had me completely flipped out.

The first time I saw her, I was walking in to work and there she was behind a register. She actually spoke to me with some dignity and respect. I was used to all those simple-minded high school broads playing me to the side. And she spoke with an experience and intellect that only an older woman could provide. Usually I'd talk to her about college and what to expect next year.

"Dag Charlie, you're doing big things, Harvard and all," she would say. "But I'm jealous, cause you'll be up there and I'll be stuck here in Durham."

She used to say stuff like that to me all the time. Finally, my silly ass started believing all those dreams she was selling me. And just like that my nosy ass Dad decided to become Super Parent.

"Charlie, you won a merit scholarship and you're accepted to Harvard," Dad tried to persuade. "So what's the attraction to Central?"

"I'm just not feeling Boston," I explained. "It gets cold up there. Anyway I like Central. They have smaller classes. It's a diverse, intimate setting."

Dad knew I was bullshitting but what could he say? Still he kept on.

"Where'd you get that from?" asked Dad. "You sound just like a brochure?"

"And you sound like you're all of a sudden ready to care about my life Dad. It's my life now; you had your chance to guide it."

"I've had responsibilities to meet Charlie, something

you'll find about soon enough! But forget all that, forget about me and your Mom for a minute. This is about you. Charlie, you have a great opportunity. That's Harvard. You graduate from there and you're set for life. Why would you throw it all away for a place like Central? Do they even have the internet there?"

"Like Central?!" I asked indignantly. "What's that supposed to mean?"

"Well, son," he said. "It's certainly no Harvard."

"You mean it's not a good school, there's too many blacks, it's too close to the bad part of town?" I asked sarcastically. "Please Dad, step into 2005. Things have changed. It's different now."

"Different? Hmm, I see," my Dad said skeptically. "Well I guess you know more than me. So there's really no sense in talking, is there? So you go to Central, but you don't have my blessing", as if it really hurt me not to have Dad's blessing.

Don't get me wrong, I loved him, but Dad didn't really know me. And as far as I was concerned, he couldn't bless what he didn't know. But one thing he said would ring prophetic.

"Dad," I said sarcastically. "Don't worry. I'll keep making those A's and without a doubt, it doesn't matter where I go to college, I'll learn to be better than you ever were."

"One thing that's sure son," he said, seeming a bit wounded by my last remark. "You're about to learn. And don't count on me or your mom to bail you out when you fall down."

I was heated. "What does he know?" I thought at the time. "And when have I ever expected them to bail me out of anything?" But in the end Dad turned out more right than he could have known. A white boy from the suburbs, I chose to step into a black world over a girl. Boy did I ever learn.

Growing up in Durham, I knew about Central, that I could get a Minority Grant-In-Aid. So paying for school wouldn't be a problem despite having to terminate my scholarship or no help from my parents. It was cool to me, like some kind of reverse affirmative action where I paid next to nothing to go to college, simply because I was white. Shit, after all was said and done, Central paid me. So I didn't have to work at all. Go figure. And even though I was white, going to Central wasn't a big deal. Of course I usually stuck with my own while in high school, but there was something about the blacks that drew me in. At the time I narrowed it to one key reason. The blacks in my school were simply more entertaining to hang with.

So my life boiled down to this. When school was in, I kept it white. But other than that, I was "hangin' with the homeys." To me, no group of people was cooler. To them, it didn't seem to matter that I was white. They made me feel more accepted, more at home than I'd ever felt around my own "friends."

Seeming to laugh at life, they had a way of cracking jokes on one another that was hilarious. And the way they poked fun at other whites cracked me up. Although they always made me feel a bit antsy when they talked like that, especially the way they bragged about fucking white girls. But they weren't including me in their jokes. I was a cool white boy, so I thought at the time. I was down. I called myself having the best of both worlds: my white friends kept me looking cool and my black friends kept me feeling cool.

Then of course there was the music. They music made being black seem like a big party-filled adventure, especially hip-hop. Those rappers lived fearlessly, calling women bitches, talking about getting high and saying "fuck the police," All this while balling out of control. I'd never heard anyone speak like that. So I used to devour hip-hop artists like Big, Jay, Pac, even the classics like N.W.A.

"Damn," my black friends would typically praise. "Look at Charlie, he knows all the words. Charlie, you ain't really white, you black ain't you?"

"Man, chill out. It's not even like that." I always said.

But on the inside, their words were music to my ears.

"Wow, I'm really down," I thought to myself. "From the way the fellas talk about most white folks, I must really be something special for them to call me black."

Really, I was the cable guy and didn't know it. Ironically, I felt my relationships with my black friends back in high school afforded me a special knowledge that made it easy to be as black as anyone. I considered myself well read. Every third Monday in January I'd religiously listen to Martin Luther King's "I Have a Dream Speech." And through the years, I'd grown to share his dream of being a white boy holding hands with a black girl, because I knew Central had some sexy-ass black girls, namely Shalese.

See, I even objectified black women the same way as my black peers. I just knew I was down. If Brother Malcolm had lived to know me, I just knew he'd have said, "Charlie's different. He's not a white devil. He's one of us. "With that outlook, I was ready for a place like central. Now being around so many black people at one time would probably be quite intimidating for most white people, but not me. I was right at home from the first day I set foot on campus. Sometimes there were awkward moments, like when I met my roommate for the first time, but I always kept it "real."

"What up dog?" I asked my roommate when we first met. "Name's Charlie, Charlie Goldberg."

"Yeah, uh, what's up? Who are you?" he asked with a skeptical tone.

"I guess I'm your roommate." I answered back to him, now looking at the nametag on our dorm room door. "You must be, uh, Reggie. Good to meet you dog."
Reggie paused for a few seconds, leaving me hanging, eagerly anticipating his dap. He must have been wondering if I was the police or not, because he just paused and sized me up. Finally, I guess Reggie decided I was cool and let down his guard.

"What the fuck," he replied. "Good to meet you man."

"Yeah, that's what's up." I said, trying to sound hip. "So, uh, you seen these bitches out here? I've never seen so many nice asses in one place at one time. These girls are probably from all over, cuz they didn't grow 'em like that in Durham."

"What you know about these black hoes Charlie?" Reggie ribbed at me.

"Well I don't know a lot," I confidently shot back, unfazed by his jab. "But you can believe if things go my way, I'll know plenty by the end of the semester."

"Ok, I hear you Charlie, I'll tell you the first place you need to go," said Reggie. "There's a pre-dawn tonight at McDougald Gym. I promise the hoes will be out."

"Word? That's what's up?"

"Yeah," Reggie said. "That's what's up; we'll really get to see what you're about Charlie."

"Don't worry Reg," I said. "I got me."

At that point I had no idea what the hell a pre-dawn was. But I couldn't let Reggie know. I figured I'd just get dressed and follow my roommate when it was time to go. Anyway, as long as Shalese was there that's all that mattered. When we got there I found out a pre-dawn was a party that lasted until the crack of dawn. They would rotate 4 D.J.'s through the night. For two hours I walked around the gym from song-to-song and finally at around 1:30 there she was. It was Shalese. The last time she saw me we had hugged goodbye before she left town for her summer break...

Shalese

I'm not trying to sound mean, because Charlie's a sweet guy, but you should have seen this boy last night at the pre-dawn party. I don't know what the hell he was trying to pull. I felt bad for him. He was trying so hard to have some flavor, but it just wasn't working. He showed up not wearing his typical faded jeans, dirty running shoes and knit polo that looked about two sizes too small for him. Nah, he was dressed for a modern day minstrel show: O.J. Simpson throwback, baggy jeans, silver chain, Timberland boots and what did it for me was that white doo rag. What the hell does a white boy need a doo rag for?!? That's kind of like a man needing a tampon. It's not like Charlie was bad looking or something, he was about 5'10", and athletic build, short brown hair, and he had medium hued brown eyes that were nicely placed over his baby face. But I could barley see all that any more. When we worked together at the Food Fresh, I'd have never thought such a straight-laced white boy could turn out like this. And just why was he at the pre-dawn anyway? I thought he'd said he had a full ride to Harvard, so what in the hell was he doing at Central of all places? I knew where I'd have had my ass right now if I'd won a scholarship to Harvard.Anyway, this fool called himself pushing up on me. I'm not one to be rude, so we talked for a minute, if you could call it that. Charlie used to be cool to talk to, but now he'd changed.

"Yo Shalese!"

At first it didn't register who he was.

"Yo," I said kinda of playing him sideways, "Charlie? Charlie is that you?"

"C'mon ma,'" Charlie said, like he was desperately trying to sound down.   "Don't even front like you don't know."

"Oh, I'm sorry, didn't recognize you at first. How are you?" I said a bit surprised to see him there, and looking like that. "Does Harvard start later than we do or something?"

"I go to school here girl."

"Really?!?" I said sounding a bit shocked. "What caused this radical move?"

"I don't know Shalese," Charlie said. "I had a change of heart."

"Well, I see the change," I said. "And I don't mean to pry, but why here?"

"What's wrong with here? Central's a good school and there's something about this place I've always loved." he said. "Anyway are you here to grill me about my life or dance."

"Is he asking me to dance?" I thought to myself. "What the hell's gotten in to Charlie? This stiff looking white boy puts on a jersey and now he thinks he's a Nigga."
The shit was funny to me, but I'm not one to be mean and it was just a dance.

"Charlie, what do you know about dancing?" I asked as we moved towards the center of the dance floor...

Charlie

I could tell Shalese was skeptical of my dancing prowless, but what she didn't know is that I'd been watching B.E.T. all afternoon. I was ready.

"I can dance," I told her. "What? You think because I'm white I can't dance. I'll rock your world girl."

"Oh really?" she asked. "Well ok then. Let's dance."

Now in retrospect I'd bitten off more than I could chew. I knew Shalese was on the dance team, meaning she could probably really move to the beat. As for me, I was never much of a dancer. My black friends in high school said I moved on the one and the three beats, that I should've been on the two's and the four's. But to me it was just a battle of mind over matter. After that, the rest was easy. So as we moved to the music, I stayed focused on one thing. I couldn't believe I was actually "getting somewhere" with Shalese. Now at first, I was real uncomfortable out there. The way a black person was able to move was always amazing to me. As for Shalese and everyone else around me, they were no different. When she first started dancing, she was moving so fast to the beat that I couldn't quite keep up. "Two's and Four's" I kept telling myself, while fighting to keep up. But the shit just wasn't working. Something had to change and fast. So I just looked at the guy next to me, and how he was dancing with his partner and bit his moves.

"Ok, yeah, I'm getting it now," I thought to myself.

Then I looked over to the guy on my left and mixed in a little of what he was doing.

"I'm really working it."

Next I decided to take all that and move in close and really show Shalese what I was working with. I had just seen my man to the right do the same thing. Ever so gracefully he'd slid down and then back up his partner's body, gyrating in slow motion as she blissfully received his gesture while continuing to move, on the two's and four's of course.

Now it was my turn to try. I moved up to her body and pressed up against her. Time to really freak her. So I dropped down, almost losing it. As I was about to fall back on my ass, I recovered catching myself with my left hand. Awkwardly, I attempted my way back up Shalese's body. Then I looked over at the guy on the right to see if I was following his move right. I focused in real hard for about 10 seconds. I was mesmerized at the way he was able to rock his pelvis with such fluid motion. As he moved, so I tried to move. Then it happened. I was rewarded. Shalese turned around finishing the rest of the song rubbing that sexy, soft ass against the vicinity of my dick.

Shalese

"What in the hell is the white boy doing?" I thought to myself. "He really thinks he's doing something. Look at how he's looking at me, like he's breaking me down or something. Yuck. Let me just turn around so I can make it through the song without laughing in his face."

You should have seen it. Charlie was off the chain. As we moved to "Candy Shop" by 50 Cent, he made a total ass of himself. What's so bad is that he didn't seem to realize it or care. I was really giving him a chance to show what he could do. I started doing my regular little jig while he swayed from side to side like a robot. His face was real intense. It looked like he wanted to fight me. I thought I saw him counting the beats. I wasn't sure about that, but it seemed like he was mumbling something. I thought I'd seen it all, but then Charlie changed it up. This guy was so unsure of what to do, and I don't think he realized I noticed but I caught him looking to the dudes to the left and the right trying to bite off of their moves. The one that did it for me was when he called himself trying to freak me. He moved in close and pressed himself against me. Then he dropped down to the floor and almost bust his ass. I was like, "What the fuck?" Finally, he lunged up from his prone position in one single gyration. The boy almost knocked me down he came back up so fast. Then he locked his eyes on the guy to his left for about 15 seconds, trying to copy him one more time. But instead of gyrating his pelvis, he was moving his torso back and forth, back and forth. He had the nerve to smile at me like he was doing something. I cracked a smile back, but really I wanted to laugh in his face. So I did what you do in moments like that, I turned my back to him. I couldn't take it anymore. And wouldn't you know, his dick got hard. Charlie was a wild dude. I wasn't mad though. Charlie may not have quite done his thing, but he didn't seem to care either. Misguided as he may have been, at least he made me laugh and helped me to have some fun until...

"Yo man! What the fuck are you looking at are you gay or something?"

"Nah," Charlie replied to the guy on the left he'd been trying to copy. "My bad."

"Your bad is right man, Don't be fuckin' checking me out like that you a faggot-ass bitch."

Poor Charlie was off to a shaky start, but that one episode wasn't enough to keep him away. I would see plenty more of him, more than I wanted for that matter...

Reggie

"Yo, he's cool man. He's cool. I got him," I said to the dude who was about to come see Charlie on the dance floor. "Charlie, man, what're you doing?"

"I really don't know," Charlie said.

"We all can see that," I told him laughing. "But don't worry about that. Let's just go before you get your ass whooped."

"Alright dog, but hold up real fast."

"Ok, but make it fast."

Charlie walked over to of all people, Shalese Lipscomb, The cutie he'd embarrassed himself with on the dance floor, the captain of the dance team, one of the baddest girls on campus.

I saw him whisper something in her ear. I thought I read her lips saying that she was sorry, but she had a boyfriend. Everyone knew that though. Shalese dated some old head, a young lawyer in his late 20's, drove a 2004 BMW 745i with 20's. All of us loved Shalese, but how the hell could we compete with that?

But getting back to Charlie, Shalese took her cell phone out and took his number. Shit, if I've seen her pull that brush off once, I've seen her pull it a million times. Then, as I expected, she smiled, gave him a peck on the check and walked off. Shot down. But I can honestly say I liked Shalese's style. She had grace about her and always knew how to let a guy off the hook without making him feel disrespected, even when he was a cornball like Charlie. But that was my room dawg. He may have showed his ass at the pre-dawn, but at least he had balls to try and fit in at Central. I don't know of too many white boys who'd have done that. Don't get me wrong, I wasn't getting soft on Charlie. The jury was definitely still out.

"What's wrong Charlie?" I asked as we walked back to the dorm.

"She's got a man" Charlie replied sighing.

"Yeah, she's got a man alright," I said. "She's got the man. He's a young hotshot lawyer working downtown. He has an office over looking the Baseball Stadium off Mangum Street and NC-147 and a hot new condo a few blocks away at the new American Campus. To top it all off, he drives a 2004 Beemer 745i."

"Come to think of it Reggie, I remember seeing him

before," Charlie said. "I think I remember seeing a dude in that car pick her up. We used to work together."

"Oh really?" I replied. "So Charlie, let me ask you something, Why is that you came here again."

"I just wanted to come here."I was still curious, so I kept prying.

"Didn't you apply other places?" I asked. "Because Central? I just don't get it."

"Well I applied to the Harvard and had a full ride, but I just wanted to stay close to home."

"So you had a full ride up North, but it was too far. I feel you. I'm from Charlotte myself, Could have gone to school in ATL, but I wanted to be closer to home too, but if not Harvard why not try to get into somewhere around here like UNC or Duke?"

Charlie just looked at me with a half smile, like he really didn't want to answer that question.

"Hold up a minute," I exclaimed with a shit-eating grin. "Please Charlie; tell me you didn't give up a full ride to go to Harvard over a bitch, a bitch you'll never even pinch."

"Ok," he said half-heartedly, knowing that I'd busted him "I didn't give up my scholarship for a bitch."

"Yooouuu dumbassss!!" I said now laughing in his face. "I mean I don't know you like that, but that's what all this is about isn't it? The doo rag, chain and Tims tell me enough, but then you pick this place over a full ride to Harvard. We get no love from the state…"

"I know right," Charlie interjected. "You should have seen the signs they used to have. Dad said they got 'em around '81 when they opened the new law school. They started off burgundy, but by 2001 they were pink. Yeah, they're doing a lot of building up now, but it'll probably be another 20 years before they do much more." I just looked at Charlie and sighed. He knew the deal and came here anyway, over a girl. There was no talking to this guy.

"I don't know about you dog. But you're cool. Still, if you think giving up a full ride to an Ivy League school impresses a girl like Shalese, then do your thing man. But you have a lot to learn about black women, shit women period."

"She was feeling me tonight, I could tell." Charlie said. "She took my number. She said we'd be friends."

By the time Charlie said that ridiculous remark, we'd made it back to our room and I was too tired to battle him any further.

"Look, you're a grown man, so I don't know what to tell you. Anyway I got to take a shower and get to bed. I'm tired as shit."

Charlie

Maybe Reggie was right. Maybe I'd made a mistake. But that morning as I lay in bed after the pre-dawn, I made a pact with myself that I'd give my best effort. I faded off to sleep replaying the night in my head, how I'd gotten to see Shalese and how I'd almost gotten my ass kicked. I knew more work had to be done in order for me to pull this off. I'd taken drama in high school. One thing I remember my instructor harping on was the value of doing research in order to get into character. That's exactly what I needed to do! With that, I closed my eyes and drifted off to sleep.

I woke up later that morning determined to study out blackness. If there was a way for a white boy to become black, I was going to find it. The first thing I did was to download song after hip-hop song from the internet. These artist's painted a bleak picture telling stories selling drugs and hurting or even killing those who got in their way. Interestingly, they called each other niggers, but I think they actually said "niggas." They glorified being thugs and referred to women with pet names like hotty, shorty, boo, babygirl, and even more disrespectful names like bitch and hoe. Most ladies loved these songs even though they insulted their womanhood. I'd never looked at it this way before, but you know, it made no difference what was being said as long as it had a catchy hook and coupled with a video resulting in a big party full of ballers.

"Is it really that easy?" I thought to myself.

I didn't buy it at first. So I dug deeper. I wanted to know why. I devoured as many rapper bios as I could find. Wouldn't you know it most of these guys rapped about poor upbringings in the hood and being trapped with no choice but to live the way they lived. They saw the American Dream in their faces every day and wanted it now. So they went after it the quickest way they knew how? No wonder so many artists pump dope. I'd have probably done it too.

After a few hours, I put it all together. My new understanding was that being black meant more than putting on a Jersey and some Tims. I had to be angry, had to be a fighter. I had to somehow capture the essence of feeling left out of mainstream society. Shit I'd been picked on from preschool through high school, so I knew something about that. And like a flash of genius, there it was. I'd figured it out. With my own "troubled past," I naturally identified with these people. My reason for attending Central became clear, to become a baller and a pimp. It was still about Shalese, but after a day of studying everything hip-hop from Def Jam to BET, I thought I'd finally found myself. I just knew I was ready and the first day of classes was just like a rubber stamp validating my overconfidence.

Reggie

After the pre-dawn, Charlie really went off the deep end. It was crazy. At one point I thought I was going to have to whoop his ass.

"Charlie, what the hell're you talking like that for?" I asked.

"Yo son! You have a problem with the way I talk?" asked Charlie in this fake-ass New York street accent.

"I don't have a problem with it, but why?" I asked.

"This is me son, this me," said Charlie.

What in the hell? This crazy ass had just looked me up and down like he wanted to come see me.

"What's up?" he asked, still sizing me up.

I was shocked at first. This guy was seriously trying to act hard. Cracking a half smile, I thought to myself, "I'd whoop his white ass, but this might be fun to watch."

"Nothing's up man, my bad." I replied. "Just curious that's all. Do your thang."

"That's what's up son," he said. "Hold me down and I hold you down."
Charlie reached out his hand to dap me up.

"Whatever, Charlie," I said returning the dap.

"Yo," said Charlie, "The name's Chucky Gee"

"Chucky what?" I couldn't believe it. Charlie had come to Central and was trying his damndest to be black. What'd Shalese do to this poor guy to make him act so foolish? But later that day he went on the yard. It was the first day of classes. I expected him to be clowned. But believe it or not, something about it worked for him. Maybe it was the shock value of it all. Maybe it was the novelty of this white kid trying so hard, but either way, most people took to him, especially the girls. The shit was amazing to me.

"Yo, Reg, Holler at ya boy." he called out to me when I bumped in to him later that day.

"What up dog?"

"What up Char, uh, I mean Chucky Gee."

"The hoes are on me dog," he said. "I should've been

doing this shit all along."

Charlie was right. This bad-assed girl came up to him and started talking.

"Aren't you in my history class that just let out?" she asked.

"Yeah, what's poppin' Shorty?"

She cracked a disbelieving laugh, like the word that fell from this wannabe's mouth didn't quite register. But after gathering herself she responded in mirroring fashion. "I'm just chillin right now. I'm Tiffany."

"Chuckie," Charlie replied. "Chucky Gee,"

Now Tiffany stood about 5'8" and combined her lanky form with amazing definition. The girl was bad. She had caramel skin, hair to her shoulders, chinky eyes, soft, moist-looking lips and long legs. Her slim build flowed outward only where necessary to form a perfect ass and 36C sized breasts that sat on her chest like those extra large navel oranges you see in the grocery store. I know he had to be nervous, but Charlie didn't blink. He just kept this hard expression on his face. Maybe she was expecting him to be your average dude and go bananas over her, but this was Chucky Gee.

"Ok, Chuckie, nice to meet you," Tiffany replied extending her hand.

"Yeah, that what's up Tiffany," Charlie said dapping her up. Now that was crazy. Charlie didn't shake this fine female's hand. He dapped her up. Tiffany just started laughing.

"Man, you're crazy" she told Charlie now passing him a slip of paper. "I just wanted to come up and talk to you though. I want you take my number. We should study sometime."

"Yeah," Charlie said. "We can study; chill out whatever you're trying to do. I'll call you."

Charlie remained so cool like Tiffany was barely even

there.

"It's like that," Reggie said. "That's what's up my Nigga."

"Reg, you know," he said. "I ain't sweating these hoes. I mean son, they so stupid. That bitch, would have played Charlie to the side. But she loves Chucky Gee, Chucky Gee's about to knock these hoes down. They don't stand a chance."

I couldn't believe how stupid these girls were to let this corny white boy pimp them like that. He was getting much love except from one in particular...

Shalese

Let me tell you about this Nigga Charlie. Well he's not really a Nigga. But I'll be damned if he's not trying. But as I was saying, that Nigga's crazy. Yesterday was the first day of class and I see him on the yard so I walk up to him to speak and he blanks on me.

"Hey Charlie," I said to him.

"Yo shorty," he said abruptly. "It's Chucky, Chucky Gee. Recognize!"

"Recognize?" I asked in disbelief. "Recognize what?"

"Charlie's soft." he said. "I'm Chucky Gee baby girl. Respect my gangsta!"

"You must be talking about your wanksta," I quickly replied, "because there's nothing about you that even smells of 'gangsta.'" Normally I'd have kept to myself. But I was getting mad at the way he was trying to play me. Unlike most of my peers, I knew the guy.

"Look Charlie, Chucky or whoever," I continued. "I don't know who you think you are. I was just coming over to speak to my friend. But if it's like that, then I'm sorry. I must've had you mistaken for someone else."

I began to walk off and Charlie quickly followed behind me.

"Hold up Shalese," he said as I was walking off. "Baby girl, it's not even like that, my bad."

"First of all, I'm not your baby girl and yeah, it is your bad," I told him as we stopped outside of Eagleton. "Central may have its share of silly bitches that'll let you talk to 'em like that, but I'm not the one. Since you've known me, I've never come off like that. And you're telling me to recognize. Recognize what? That you were just plain disrespectful? I recognize that. What's with this crazy act?"

"C'mon girl," he said. "It's not even like that. This the real me, so take it how you wanna take it. I'm about to be out. One."

I couldn't believe Charlie. Where'd he get off and just what was he trying to prove anyway? He may have been getting play from these other stupid broads, but I wasn't the one...I was so perplexed that I almost missed my cell phone ringing. It was Jason.

"Hey baby, how are you?...Oh really your working late?...Well I was looking forward to seeing you, but ok...I know you've got a lot on you, but Friday you're all mine....Ok, I love you Jason...Bye"

Jason was the kind of guy for a lady to want. He was a lawyer. Everything about him smelled of success. When I met Jason a couple of years back, he'd just finished law school, taken his bar and set up shop in town. Back then he was just another cute face with potential. But I could tell he was going places and believe me, he's gone places since that time. My baby came to Durham and hit the ground running. In a year he went from driving an old Toyota to flossing a 745i Beemer. You know, I really wanted to see my baby that night but how could I have faulted him for being on his grind. He had a condo, his condo with his payment. To me, that said a lot. See I wasn't trying to be your average silly young girl. I cared about my future. So the choices I made were important to me, all the way down to the man I dated. He had to be more than someone who made me feel good all the time. He had to be about success and having something. Hell that Nigga might be my husband one day, the father of my kids. I didn't see myself as choosing style over substance. I did that once back in high school and he turned out to be sorry. But I learned. I saw no upside in that. The next time, I wasn't gonna settle for any of that fake gangster bullshit. So then Charlie Goldberg, the bag boy, comes to Central playing the part and thinks he's gonna get some play, hell no, even if I didn't already have a man. He surprised me the most. That boy had it all. I guess even Charlie's wasn't immune to seeing one too many music videos.

Charlie

Shalese was right. I was disrespectful. I just didn't see it that way at the time. I was getting too much love. After a few weeks, I'd made it. I'd become Chucky Gee. All over campus, I became known as this crazy white boy, crazy enough to choose a street life over the suburbs. What's really wild is that everyone bought it, so just like that I had what's known as "street cred." As far as everyone knew, I was selling in other cities like Burlington and Greensboro, which was a lie. But I didn't tell it. You know how people like to talk. Help keep the lie going, I took all that speculation and ran. I didn't want to seem to big so I had my Altima tricked out. It was an '05, a graduation gift. With my refund check money, it was nothing to get some rims, a system and tinted windows. Next, I gave Reggie the money to cop me some heat from the pawnshop. Being 18, I was too young to do that. With that, the transformation was completed. In my own mind, I'd become a self-made black man and no one could tell me shit.

Of course, the harder I seemed, the more Tiffany was feeling me, so we became friends, There'd be times she'd use her Mom's credit card to set me straight with the hottest gear. Academik Sean John, Rockawear, you name it. We'd talk on the phone a lot. And I hadn't even fucked yet. But I knew she wanted me. Something had to give. But I was scared.

Ever since I was a boy every reliable source, from comedians to jokers in the locker room, had confirmed that black guys had big dicks and knew how to fuck and that black women had to have it and it better be freaky and done right.

"Damn," I thought to myself. "Black people sure love their sex."

That's what I'd heard up to that point, so that's what I believed. To back me up, I thought about all the records R. Kelly sold after peeing on that girl. So I was like,   "Shit   I need to piss on bitches too." What really threw me was learning that even the Reverend Dr. King would take a break from it all to get freaky with someone besides the Mrs. I always saw myself as a pretty horny guy, but Dr. King did his thing.

"I'm no doctor and I'm certainly no reverend," I thought to myself. "My shit's only six inches, hard. How do I measure up to that?"

I knew had to find an edge to get on Tiffany's level.

"Welcome to the Naughty Shop," the sales lady said. "Just let me know if there's something I can do to help you."

"Uh, Thanks" I said. "I do have a question."

"Ok."

"Yeah, I'm getting with this girl, I think she's a super freak," I continued, "Do you have anything I can use to keep up with her? You know stamina and all?"

"I've got the perfect thing for you," she said pulling

down this blue box labeled "Ready." "Here this pill will make you harder than ever and it'll make you last for hours. I promise you she won't know what hit her, but you only need one 30-60 minutes prior to the act."

"Ok," I said. "That's what's up."

After that, all I had to do was get over to Tiffany's to "study."So I called her up.

"Tiff, yo what up ma," I said, "This Chucky, Chucky Gee."

"Oh hey Chucky," she said, "What's up player."

"Chillin, Chillin, you know how I do," I told her. "So what's up with History? You know our first test is coming up. We should go ahead and study a little."

"Ok," she said. "We can do that."

"You hungry Tiff?" I asked.

"Yeah, a little," she said "You hungry now?"

"Yeah we'll eat before we study."

"Ok Charlie, so come thru whenever you're ready."

I could tell by how quickly she agreed to everything that the last thing on her mind was studying. So there was no need to go all out. When in Rome, right? So I took her down Fayetteville Street to this low budget spot called "Church's" and ordered a 12-piece box and a half gallon of iced-tea for eight dollars.

Maybe she was expecting a trip to a nice restaurant, and Charlie Goldberg would have done just that, but this was Chucky Gee and Chucky Gee was fucking tonight.

Next we went back to her apartment and ate. I pulled out a blunt, something I'd never done.

"Yo Tiff," I said. "I can't study without getting high first. I'm about to blaze."

"Ok," she said

With that, I lit up the blunt, inhaled one deep breath and started gagging. I gagged so hard that I upchucked my chicken dinner all over Tiffany's coffee table. Luckily she was in the back using the bathroom, so she didn't come out right away.

I had to move fast. Scrambling to the kitchen, I found some paper towels and a plastic mixing bowl. Quickly, I wiped the warm puke into the bowl and sprayed the glass table top down with cleaner I'd found. Not wanting to pour the puck down her kitchen sink, I wrapped it up to make it look like leftovers I was taking with me. If Tiff hadn't been in the back, she'd have probably been turned off. So I was glad she was taking so long. I got all cleaned up the nick of time. But it wasn't over there. Those "Ready" pills from the sex store were about to do their thing. The directions said take one, but I'd taken five. I had rise to the occasion. But what a huge mistake that was. Literally I had to learn my lesson the hard way.

"Chuckie, what you smoking on in there," she asked. "I might need to hit that shit the way it had you gagging."

"Ok ma," I said. "Do your thing."

She came out of the bathroom, wearing some cute boy shorts and a tank top. Her hair was now taken down and it gently cascaded to her shoulder. That body was so tight. As she moved closer, I really noticed the contrast between her flat stomach and her protruding 36C breasts. Then she turned to sit beside me and I saw the way her apple ass shaped those boy shorts. Then her legs, those long legs looked so soft. In all, she was looking so good and smelling so sweet, like some flowery lotion.

All of a sudden my dick was hard, harder than it had ever been before. Was this supposed to be happening to me? Maybe I'd taken too many pills. Then I started sweating profusely and started feeling light-headed.

"Chuckie you don't look too good." I faintly heard Tiffany saying. "You need something."

"I'm good ma," I said.

"Chuckie!!..."

I don't know what happened after that but I must have passed out because the next thing I know, I woke up in the ER with my dick still as hard as a rock.

"Mr. Goldberg, good to see you back with us," the female doctor said. "We had to pump your stomach."

"Whatever you took," she added now looking towards the tent poking up from my pelvic area, "uhh, we weren't able to get it all."

"I don't know what happened." I offered with some embarrassment. "But it won't happen again."

After getting dressed and walking out to the waiting room, there was Tiffany in a bit of disarray, but she was there. If she'd known why I'd ended up in the hospital, she'd have probably let me overdose. I didn't want to tell her what had happened, but on the way home, she wouldn't stop talking to me.

"Chuckie, are you ok?" she asked.

"I'm fine now ma," I said, "Thanks for asking, thanks for getting me to the E.R."

"No problem boo," she said with a chuckle as she glanced towards my pelvis region. "Anything to help a friend out of a hard situation."

"Oh so you have jokes," I said. "Very funny, I could have died and you're laughing."

"I'm laughing at how crazy that was." She said. "You may not remember, but it was a time getting you to the car, you kept trying to kiss on me and feel on my titties, and while we were on the way to the ER, you kept rubbing on my legs. I must've had to pop your hand 10 times while I was driving. What the fuck were you on Charlie?"

"Look ma!" I said trying to sound extra hard, real, or whatever it was supposed to be. "What the fuck!?! I got sick. Why you fucking with me?"

"I'm just concerned Chuckie," she said. "You had me scared."

Not wanting to tell her the real deal, I amped on her.

"You know what, just let me out here." I said. "I'll fuckin' walk. You don't know me like that, asking all those fuckin' questions."

So Tiffany pulled the car to the side of the road.

"Ok motherfucker," she said. "You wanna act all hard then get the fuck out!"

"Aight," I said. "That's what's up. I'll get out. I'm Chuckie-mother-fucking-G.   What?"

Tiffany drove off upset and there I was standing alone on Fayetteville Street about 10 blocks from school after dark with my truly white ass. This was part was truly the Hood, so I was scared. I figured I should continue the role. It worked at Central, so why wouldn't it work in the Hood? As Tiffany pulled off, I noticed a car that had just passed as it stopped and turned around. When the car made it to where I was standing, it stopped. I was at the corner of this housing community called Fox Gate.

"My Nigga," a voice called out from the early 90's Nissan Sentra. "I need a favor, I need to hold $1, I'm about to run out of gas. Can you get me?"

"Well," I thought to myself. "He did call me 'my Nigga.'"

So I reached in for my wallet.

"Here my Nigga," I said back to him. "Here's five."

Next thing I know this motherfucker pulled a pistol on me. "My Nigga you've got balls that's for sure," he said. "For one thing you're out alone on this side of town this time of night. Nigga what the fuck is you thinkin'? And then you go and call me your Nigga. I told you you're my Nigga, so how can I be your Nigga? Now empty your wallet and those Force Ones, let me get them too."

This wasn't good. Clearly he didn't mean I was his Nigga in the brotherly kind of way. As soon as I handed over my money and gear he said. "Ooo your dick hard. Yous a nasty Nigga. There's kids' living in these houses."Next thing I know, the guy shot me in the shoulder."Watch your back cracker!!" he yelled out the window before he sped off. "Take your ass back to Hope Valley!!"

Shalese

I remember that night like it was yesterday, and for more reasons than Charlie Goldberg. But I'll get to that later. Anyway, I was heading down Fayetteville Street towards Jason's apartment. I was going to surprise him with a special dinner. The next thing I know I see this white boy rolling over on the side of the rode. As I got closer, I could see it was Charlie. I know he'd become this silly-assed-jerk but I couldn't just leave him there.
I parked behind him to protect him from oncoming traffic and to shine the headlights on him. Getting out of the car, I walked to over.

"Charlie are you ok?" I asked him.

"Shalese," he said breathing with noticeable discomfort. "It's Chucky Gee. What you doing here ma?"

There he was, still trying too hard. I wanted to leave him there for being so fake, but I couldn't do that. So I just went along with his crazy talk so I could coax him to the car.

"I should be asking you that Charlie," I said. "Do you need any help?"
When Charlie rolled over to look at me, I was horrified to see his left hand clenching his bloodied right shoulder. He was about to speak. But I stopped. (Thinking)

"Oh my God Charlie, what did you do!?!" I exclaimed. "You've been shot!"

He didn't have much of a response except for repeating some crazy line. "He wasn't my Nigga, I was his Nigga,"

I didn't want to know what he was talking about; I just knew he needed a doctor and fast.

"Look Charlie," I said. "Save your breath, don't speak. I'm taking you to Duke Hospital. Don't worry."

"It's Chucky Gee," his crazy ass replied as I helped him to the car.

I was worried because he'd lost of a lot of blood and was acting loopy, and for some reason his dick was hard. I'd never known that to be an affect from getting shot. Anyway, Duke was only a few minutes down the road. All I had to do was get on 147 and I'd be there.

What in world had poor Charlie gotten himself into? Who in the hell did he think he was walking in the hood after dark anyway? He'd probably gotten his stupid ass robbed. In a way it served him right for trying to front like that, but nah, no one deserves that to happen to 'em.

The bullet must have gone through his back because I had blood on my sleeve from where I helped him to his car. I thought he might be going into shock so I stepped on it.

"Hang in there Charlie," I tried to reassure him. "Don't worry baby."

"Chucky Gee," he slurred out. "Not worried, Happy to see you."
Oh shit this Nigga was really losing it he'd just been shot and he's trying to hola.

"God please watch over Charlie," I prayed to myself. "He may be shallow, but c'mon he's 18, who isn't shallow at 18. Please God, it's not his time, it's not his time. That's all I can say Lord. Amen"After doing 90 mph on NC-147 and then running all the stoplights from the Fulton Street exit to Duke Hospital, we finally made it to the Emergency Room.I jumped out and ran into the Triage area.

"I need help outside," I yelled out. "My friend's been shot and lost a lot of blood."

Two nurses flew up from what they were doing and came outside to assist Charlie. Then something crazy happened, something unexpected. As they were wheeling Charlie away he reached his left arm across his body. Clenching his bloodied hand to my wrist, he motioned me closer.

"I didn't go to Harvard," he whispered barley audible, "because I wanted to get close to you."

"You wanted to what?" I asked because I wasn't making him out clearly.

"Get close to you," he said again, but still it didn't quite register.

"Huh," I asked one more time.

"Ma'am," a nurse said. "We need to get him inside. Don't worry we'll take good care of your boyfriend."

"Oh he's not my boyfriend." I quickly replied. "He's just a friend."

Like that really mattered at such a time, but I was too stuck on what that crazy white boy had just told me. They rolled him away and I stood outside stunned. I was about to go inside I just needed to gather my thoughts. I began to cry for Charlie. I'd known him for about a year and that he was better than how he'd been acting. And if I had just heard him right, he did it all because of me. I know I sound weak, but I felt somewhat responsible. Now I'd been outside a minute and was about to gather myself and go back inside, but then there he was. I just stared in shock as he walked by me. It was Jason wearing a wedding band and escorting this pregnant woman and a toddler thru the door. The woman looked like she was in labor. Most women would have blanked seeing all that, but I was raised to be bigger. Don't get me wrong, I was hurt but it was completely obvious that it was me who was the other woman. So I just stood there and kept my cool as he walked right past me like I wasn't even there.

I made damn sure Jason was inside, and after that I casually walked to my car, opened the door and sat inside. As soon as I closed the door, the tears started flowing. I know I should have stayed to check on Charlie. But I had to get out of there. I just rode up and down campus drive between Duke's East and West campuses, sobbing my heart out.

First there was the shock of seeing Charlie Goldberg being close to death from being shot and then now me feeling like I'd just died.

"How could he play me like that?" I asked myself. Then I thought of that woman and that little boy. "He had a wedding band on, were they his kids? Damn he seemed so perfect? What'd I do to deserve this?"Seriously, I didn't understand why. But as I continued to cry my way back and forth between the two sides of campus, I thought about Charlie and how he ended up in the hospital. Something connected. I realized that I'd been just as shallow as him.

"This is stupid," I said to myself. "I need to get back and check on my friend."
So I turned from Campus Drive on to Anderson and headed back to the hospital resolved that it wasn't just Chucky Gee whose bubble had been burst.

Charlie

"Wow, what a day." I thought to myself as I came to from my surgery. I'd been to the hospital twice. And being shot really scared me. "Who in the hell have I become?" I thought as I came to consciousness.

"Fuck love." I mumbled not aware Shalese was waiting beside me in the recovery room. The doctors had let her
back to sit with me.

"That's not a nice thing to say Charlie," she said.

"Shalese," I responded. "You didn't have to wait with
me, where are my parents?"

"Well, you don't have your wallet; I guess it was stolen
so no one knew how to call your parents. You'd have had to
wait here all alone," she said "Something tells me that you
wouldn't have left me like that, so here I am."

"I appreciate that," I said.

"You're welcome," she replied. "So why 'fuck love'
Charlie?"

"Uh, well, I didn't know you were in the room," I said.
"It's kind of personal."

"Ok then Charlie, I guess I'll just pretend I didn't hear
that, just like I didn't hear that confession of yours before they
rolled you into the ER," she said.

"Huh?"

"Yeah that's right," she replied. "You had me saying
the same thing."

"Shalese, when I said that, I thought I was dying," I
responded.

"That's cool, no need to explain, I'm not gonna to
blow up your spot, that's between me and you," she said
before pausing to hit me with a coy smile. "But there's one
thing. I just have a proposal."

"Proposal?" I asked. "What's up?"

"Let's just say I've been thinking that maybe we got
off on the wrong foot and I was thinking maybe we could
start over," she said. "I know you're probably wondering
where all this is coming from. But I've been thinking we've
both been wrong here."

"What are talking about Shalese?" I asked. "I thought

you had someone."

"Look Charlie don't worry about all that," she said. "Just listen to the doctors and get healed and the next time you see me out and about, if you want, ask me for my number again... And I'm not proposing any of this to Chucky Gee, it's for Charlie Goldberg, my favorite bagger. Ok?"I wasn't sure if I was more shocked from being shot or from Shalese's radical change of heart. I must admit that part of me was eating this up."So why the change of heart Ms. Lipscomb?" I asked while mirroring back the same coy smile she'd flashed me.

Shalese calmly laughed. "Charlie, don't think I don't notice you eating all this up," she said, now pausing, and sounding a bit more somber, even with a slight tremble to her voice. "For right now, let's just say that you had your reason for turning down your scholarship and I have mine for my change of heart. Ok?"

"Ok," I said. "I'll keep that in mind."

"Oh yeah," she remembered. "Here I brought you something"

Shalese handed me a copy of *Souls of Black Folks* by W.E.B. Dubois.

"Thanks Shalese," I said. "That's real thoughtful."

"No problem Charlie," she said. "Read it. Ok? I'll see you around."

"And Oh yeah," I said, "Thank's for saving my life Shalese."

"Your welcome," she said and then continued to joke. "But you need to quit hanging with that Chucky Gee fellow, he's trouble."

"I think you're right," I conceded back to her.

After Shalese left the recovery area I was alone. It was just me and the *Souls of Black Folks.* I opened the book and found an inscription from Shalese.

Charlie,
    May the words in this book bless you with a deeper understanding. This material is not for the faint of heart. But I've never pegged you as fainthearted.
Always,
Shalese.

I found a page that she'd tabbed for me with a high-lighted passage. It was as if Dubois spoke directly to my soul when he wrote, "After the Egyptian and Indian, the Greek and Roman, the Teuton and Mongolian, the Negro is a sort of seventh son, born with a veil, and gifted with second-sight in this American world, — a world which yields him no true self-consciousness, but only lets him see himself through the revelation of the other world. It is a peculiar sensation, this double-consciousness, this sense of always looking at one's self through the eyes of others, of measuring one's soul by the tape of a world that looks on in amused contempt and pity. One ever feels his twoness, — an American, a Negro; two souls, two thoughts, two un-reconciled strivings; two warring ideals in one dark body, whose dogged strength alone keeps it from being torn asunder."

After reading that, I was broken. I'd had no idea what I was doing. How could I have known? But after that, I knew that by creating Chucky Gee, I'd ignorantly imposed this principle on the people around me, Reggie, Shalese, everyone.

I cried that night. But it was good because, for the first time, my eyes were opened. By no means was I healed of my ignorance, but now I knew now why I'd been shot. That guy who robbed me was an ignorant motherfucker, but I called him "my Nigga" while walking in his part of town where I knew no one. And that's where the shit hit the fan. I realized

I'd made myself into this media manufactured thug. Where everyone at Central let that shit go, this guy read through me and let me know his dissatisfaction, not that he should have shot me but I understood better why he did it.

Like I said in the beginning, love makes you do some crazy shit. I'd done all this because that's what I thought would get me Shalese. Really I'd lived a lie. Yet now Shalese was proposing a fresh start. But why?

Shalese

That night when Charlie was shot and I saw Jason with his family, yes my eyes were opened about Charlie's heart and Jason's sorry ass. But I also saw myself. Before I'd always thought of myself as graceful and entitled to the best my charms could get me. That's still true. But before that night at the hospital, I'd have never given the Charlie Goldberg's of this world a chance. See, my notions of manhood weren't mine. From images in magazines, to TV, to movies, to your name, all my life I was force-fed that the ideal man was simply a baller. So Jason didn't have me at hello. He had me the first time he rolled up beside me in that chromed out 745i. I see it now. I was no different than all the girls who flipped out over Chucky Gee. My Chucky Gee was a bit more sophisticated, but in the end all he turned out to be was the same lie Charlie told. The only difference, Jason wore designer suits.

Getting back to Charlie, we bumped into each other a few weeks later. He was looking so cute. He still wore an urban look, some Air Force Ones and cream Sean John jumpsuit. But there was something more regular about him, something real. I guess you could say, the first time all year I saw Charlie Goldberg.

CONCRETE JUNGLE

Charlie

There she was walking out of the library. It was still early in the semester, meaning it was still warm. She wore some Khaki Capri's that hugged her hips and these cute open-toe sandals with a colorful spaghetti string top. Boy she was doing it that day. Needless to say, I was nervous not having Chucky Gee around. But what the hell right?

"Hey Shalese," I called out. "What's up?"

She was playing that fresh start to the max. Again, it was grace that made her so beautiful. So I just played right along.

"I go to school here now."

"Oh really?" she said coyly. "But I thought you had a full ride? What on earth would make you give up a full ride to Harvard to come to Central of all places?"

"I have my reasons," I said smiling confidently, "Maybe if you give me your number we can talk about that more. Ok?"

"Charlie, did I ever tell you I like your style?" she asked me while writing something on a scrap of paper. "Here, call me; we'll have to talk about those reasons. But right now I'm late for class."

"Yeah, I'll do that," I said. "It's good seeing you again."

"I must agree Charlie," she said. "I'm glad to see you're here at Central."

Understanding that it was her way of letting all the past bull shit go, I just smile at her cute little act. After that, the rest was history.

Shalese and I have been dating for a few months. It hasn't always been easy. A lot people don't understand what we have and hate but that's ok. We know why we're together. Shit happens I guess. But when our shit happened, we finally looked for our answers from within ourselves and stopped living in search of Chucky Gee.

Joe Margolis lives in Charlotte, NC. Margolis attended the University of North Carolina at Chapel Hill. He graduated in 2001 with a degree in Journalism and Mass Communication. He's freelance written for local news media and prior to that he's always been a writer at heart. He is busy at work on his own novel entitled "Traded All." You can reach him through email at J_Margolis@hotmail.com

Birth Of
A Hustler

| Nikia Comfort

The story starts at the end of the 80's. Our 26-year-old mother, Donna, is a caramel complexioned shapely woman standing 5'9"with big, light brown eyes like one of those spider monkeys. Her locks sit in bouncy, loose, pressed curls about her shoulders. She has a scar the size of a nickel on the side of her face from the doctor trying to remove her from the womb during a breach birth. She carries a look of undeniable confidence on her face and with that manner she glides, as if on water, when she walks. She works as a nurse at the Graduate Hospital, and our father, Clarence, works for the city's sanitation unit, in addition to his under the table money-making antics. Clarence was another story. Dad was dark, melted chocolate brown he stood about 6'4" and was as massive in appearance as Andre the Giant to us. He had 'good hair' as they say, an attribute I was blessed with, and had a pretty boy face that changed like a mood ring when he was displeased. Despite his pretty boy looks, he was one of the most intimidating, 'don't fuck with me' men I'd ever come across. Despite being a loving father, he was scarier than the boogieman when his disposition changed to discontent.

Both of them were raised on the streets. They lived in a moderately large corner row home in South West Philadelphia. The large brick exterior of the home appears complete with patio furniture secured to the porch with chains. The large picture window is adorned with vases full of silk flowers and outlined with cream cotton and sheer curtains. The walls of the living room are adorned with pictures of my brother and me. They were having another red light card game in the basement.

This party was a normal weekly event. Every Friday at around 10 or 11 at night, some of Mom and Dad's friends would come over for as long as I could remember. The parties normally would run into the morning involving high price drinking, ghetto fabulous liquors and various drugs. Quintin, my brother, was as thin as a rail, a little darker then our father, and the splitting image of him. He was tall for his age. He was blessed with my dad's 'Jolly Green Giant' genes. Me, I was tall for my age, I guess. I had my father's 'good' hair, my mother's big glowing eyes, and what must have been grandma's weight because I was a bit on the round side Quintin and I crept down from the second story from our bedrooms, which were carefully selected in the rear of the house. We could smell the scent of mom's vanilla incense and some shit they be smokin "called killa", It stinks. As we moved closer to the kitchen and near the basement door we could hear 'Give It to Me Baby' by Rick James blaring over the speakers... As Quintin pushes the colorful, hippie, afro-centric beaded divider behind the doorway to the side there it was:Mom said, "Don't make me come up there and kick y'all ass; its 12 o'clock. Take ya asses to bed!"

"Damn"! We took off running when we heard that. I don't know how she does it. I swear we were quiet. Quintin pushed me into the adjoining wall in the kitchen and ran around running back up the stairs that we just came down. I said to my brother, "Like it's my fault, you know she got powers." (As I put my hands out in front of me, walking like a zombie).Quintin replies, "Dummy."

Dad is at a card table in the middle of the floor throwing his cards down. He bellows, "Now mu'fucka, waz' up Turk. Gimme my $10." Mom starts to laugh as she brings Dad a beer from the refrigerator. She places it on the table with the weed, coke, and pills that sat on individual mirrors, where the card pot usually is. While rubbing dad's shoulders Mom says, "You winning baby? Kick they ass." A voice from the corner of the basement said, "Donna, can you pass me a beer? "Mom looked to another corner of the basement, where the crap game is being played. She nods her head and rolls her eyes as she turns around mumbling, "I ain't no maid. Y'all got legs or you better start tipping. What the fuck you think this is. Self serve!"

The party lasted well into the morning. People came and people went. The noise grew as people became more and more intoxicated. Occasionally, a fight broke out. Nothing too severe, just somebody drunk and running off at the mouth. The altercation usually ended with them being thrown out into the street by father. We would usually stay upstairs and play Atari, watch TV and movies until our eyes closed. Mom didn't bother us too much as long as we stayed out of sight.

On Saturdays Mom would take us into town to the Gallery or to Chestnut St. to shop and see a movie. This was the usual family outing for Saturday. Dad usually worked around the house or ran whatever errands he needed to get out of the way. Usually it was working around the house on Mom's 'Honey Do' list. In the evening we would rent movies and sit around together watching them, or Dad would take us skating at Elmwood. Those were the days. Repetitive, normal, usual; notice the repetition of the word, it is not an accident. There weren't many surprises for us then.

Everything was taken care of for us. It's quite amazing how a series of events that threatens to change, your life, your outlook, can stem from one incident. I don't think that you fully grasp the importance of making well thought out decisions until the action is an afterthought. Usually at this point it's too late, ergo 'afterthought'. The damage has already been done; you just don't know it yet. It would be great if you could go back in time and take back all of those things that you felt you'd done wrong and redo them wouldn't it, but that would change the whole meaning of life. Anyway....

One night mom sent Quintin to the corner store for some last minute stuff for dinner, a soda and cornbread or something. The corner store on our block had just closed, so he headed to the Chinese mini mart around the corner and down the block. As he walked past an alley down the street from the closed store an old-head, smoker snatched him up and pulled him into the alley. The guy that grabbed him searched his pockets and took the money mom had given him. It was only a few dollars but Quintin didn't want mom and dad to think he lost or spent the money on dumb stuff. Quintin knew the guy from around the neighborhood.

Quintin started bitchin', telling the guy to leave him alone and give him the money back, "Stop playing. Get off. Give me my money back. What you doin'? I'm tell my dad."The guy punched Quintin twice in the gut and slapped him around, then threw him to the ground and stepped off. Quintin got home a few minutes later. He had a cut over his eye and a big lip. He was holding his stomach. Mom started screaming and crying as soon as she saw him. She rushed to his side to kiss his boo-boos.

Dad yelled from the couch, "What happened? Who the fuck did this? Those little bastards down the street jumped you?"
Quintin responded shyly with, "It was Koota. He snatched me in the alley and took the money. I tried to get it back and he hit me. I wasn't a punk dad, I wasn't. I swear I wasn't no punk."

Mom shot Dad a dirty look when Quintin said that. When Dad thought he knew who the guy was, he made a couple of phone calls, ran upstairs to get his gun, it was a shiny chrome 380 and grabbed his Louisville slugger out of the closet. Mom followed him, foot to foot, around the house. When Dad grabs that bat you knew it was problems. Mom pleaded, "Please just let the police handle it. Just call the police!!!"

Quintin was more worried about what was going to happen than the fact that he looked like Kid Dynomite. Dad left. Mom waited up that night, playing Minnie Riperton's Perfect Angel album all night, smoking joints, and drinking beer. Every five minutes she would pick up the phone antici-pating its ring. Dad didn't come home until the next morning. He had a different shirt on and blood on his boots. Mom asked Dad about that night but he wouldn't discuss it. Later the next day we were all called to the dining room.
Dad had his hands together and his head down as he called to us, "Come sit down everybody. Look don't any of you say anything about this to anyone. If anybody asks you what happened, tell them you were in a fight. You understand! You were in a fight. We don't talk about this night again. I

mean that, never again."We never talked about that night again and Quintin never saw Koota again, none of us did. And life just went on like usual.

The following summer, shit started falling apart as it often tends to do. Dad was not working again but he was making a killing in whatever he was doing on the side. Mom had found some chick's number named Candi's in the house. She was washing clothes and found it in a pair of Dad's pants on a match cover. Here we go. "The Drama..."Mom says as sweet as pie while shooting Dad a dirty look, "Babe, who the fuck is Candi? I found some bitch named Candi's number in a pair of your pants. Who the fuck is she?"

Never looking away while laying on the couch watching TV, Dad responded, "What? Donna, I don't know what you talking a bout. I don't know no damn Candi. Throw the number away if it's bothering you so much. Go head with that shit."Mom did throw the number away, but she knew that wasn't the end of it.

The shit you do in the dark always comes to light...Mom was taking Quintin and me to get some ice cream a few weeks later. Dad was supposed to be looking for work. On the way back from the ice cream store. Mom decided to make a few stops. One of them was near one of Dad's spots. Who does she see sitting on the corner but Dad all hugged up with some lady. Now we saw it too, but from the look on Mom's face with all those lines in her forehead and the way she gripped the steering wheel like she was squeezing the juice out of an orange, we knew not to dare say a word. By the time Dad got home that night, Mom had thrown all of his clothes and stuff out the window onto the curb.

Dad started yelling while pulling up to the house, "What the fuck is this shit? Donna, Donna you done lost ya damn mind." As he walks in, he calmly says to my mom, "Baby, Why's all my shit in the street? You better get my shit up out the street woman."

Mom yelled, "Fuck you, ya lying bastard. Tell me you looking for work while you out sportin some ho ass bitch. Pick ya shit up and take it to ya ho. Let her wash your clothes, cook your food, suck your dick and the rest of the shit I gotta deal with. While you go and fuck some ho, please. Nigga get the fuck out of my face."

Needless to say after a few more verbal exchanges, shit got physical. Dad smacked Mom like she stole something from him and she fell on the living room couch like a ton of bricks. Then the tears started. As Quint and I sat at the top of the steps, we knew all hell was getting ready to break loose. The last time my father hit my mother, she poured boiling water on his feet and whipped his ass. We went upstairs to call Aunt Jo, mom's best friend and our god-mother. Jo was mom's best friend since they were little kids. Jo was portly and short. She had a short mini fro of tight curls and wore wire frame glasses. She had never been married and didn't have any kids.

While we called, we heard cussing and breaking of lamps, dishes, and vases as they moved from the living room to the kitchen. Mom had just pulled a knife when there was a knock at the door. It was the police. Dad had backed his way to the door while keeping an eye on Mom as he answered it; Mom was still going off. Aunt Jo got there soon after. The police persuaded Dad to leave for the night. I don't think he was going to, but when Mom swore, "Ya ass ain't getting no sleep up in this mu'fucka tonight, ya bitch." He knew it was time to go, mom was not playing games.A few days later he came back with gifts, flowers and stuff talking about how sorry he was. They headed up to the bedroom. Needless to say shit went OK for a little while.

A week later, when we got home from school, mom started cooking dinner. Aunt Jo popped up to help cook. Quintin and I were in the living room playing Atari when there was a "Knock, knock, knock" at the door. Why is it Candi, Dad's girlfriend/mistress, wanting to talk to my Mom (bad idea)? Poor girl must either be dumb or crazy. She was about 5'10" and looked rather young. If I had to guess, I'd say she was about 22. At least Dad had good taste in side pussy. She was rather busty and had hips and booty for days. She was wearing a white mini dress that stopped about 4 inches above her knee and a pair of opened toe white pumps. Mom invited her in to talk and chased us upstairs. You could start to see those lines in her forehead again saying:' This bitch got a lot of nerve' all over my mom's face despite her calm demeanor.

Mom told me and Quintin, "Y'all go up to your room and shut the door. I'll call you for dinner."

Mom and Candi introduced themselves and Mom asked her to have a seat on the couch. Jo is ear-hustling in the kitchen. Candi starts telling Mom that she has been messing with Dad for over a year and that she's been to the house before with him. Now mom's face went to Not in my house. She showed Mom a ring he had bought for her that was caked with diamonds at least 3 carats, did you understand caked? She claimed that she felt Mom had a right to know. She said that he had promised her he was leaving Mom and they were going to start a family. Needless to say, after the flashing of the ice, Mom snapped and went off. Fucking was one thing, but he was spending 'OUR' money on her, that set it off like the 4th of July.

Mom said in a very cool, calm and collected tone, "I appreciate you coming to me and all to tell me this. But, bitch, you must be crazy coming to my house telling me how you fucking my husband, not some nigga, not my boyfriend, not just some dick I get, my mu'fuckin husband. And then you gonna say you been in my house. You're trifling for coming to some other bitches' house with her man, why didn't you take him home? So what you done fucked in my shit, my shit, where I lay my fucking head and raise and feed my kids. Now I got to burn the mu'fuckin' bed. Who the fuck do you think you are?"

She smacked the shit out of Candi (we knew because we could hear it all the way up stairs) for having the nerve to tell her how she's breaking up her family and then the shit hit the fan. As we were running down the steps to see the commotion and get good seats, Aunt Jo grabbed us and took us to the kitchen as she told us, "Un-un. In the kitchen. I mean it, stay there."

Our Dad couldn't have worse timing. He parks the car that nice black Thunderbird looking like he just came from the car wash, as he walks up to the house he can hear the noise. Dad says to the neighbors as he approaches with a puzzled expression, "Get out of here, and come on now. Move." As he urges the neighbors away he continues with, "What the hell y'all circling my house for."

When he came through the front door he saw Mom and Aunt Jo jumping Candi. We were on the love seat cheering Mom and Auntie on like we were watching the Eagles football game. Dad tried to break it up, wondering what the hell Candi was doing at the house in the first place. Mom kicked him in the nuts, taking him down, when he tried to get in between them. Auntie kept on whipping on Candi. Mom ran and got Dad's gun while he was down. She started pointing it at him, trippin. I mean she looked like her head was gonna spin and everything. We got scared and I started crying, again. Mom told us to go upstairs.Mom yelled, "Go upstairs, NOW! (Waving the gun) So bitch (looking toward Dad), you don't know no Candi. You leaving me huh mu'-

fucka. In a fucking box maybe. Get the fuck out!!! Get the fuck out!!!"

Mom led Dad to the door at gunpoint and put him out, locking the door behind him. Candi started screaming uncontrollably expecting the worst. That's when we peeked down from the top of the steps.Dad yelled from the porch, "Now Donna you need to calm down now, you acting crazy." Mom, still yelling with the gun to Candi's head, "Bitch strip! That's what you do ain't it. Ain't it! Strip!"Candi cried, "NO, no. Please don't kill me. I'm sorry. I'm sorry. I didn't know, I didn't know."Mom yelled back, "Bitch strip before I blow ya fucking head off. (Clicking the gun) And take that mutha-fucking ring off. I'm sure some of my money went up into that."Aunt Jo tried to intervene, "Uh, Donna. Donna. Don't you think this is getting out of control?"Mom gave Jo a look waving the gun and plainly said, "Shut up Jo."

Aunt Jo put her hands up in the air and backed off. She just let mom go on and hoped for the best. With her hands still up, palms out in a defensive manner, she uttered with resilience, "OK".

Candi started to take off her clothes, crying more and more as she removed each piece of clothing. Mom directed Aunt Jo to get a trash bag and put all of her clothes in it. When she was totally naked, Mom led her to the door with the gun to her head, steady yelling obscenities, and put her out on the porch as she said to our Dad, "Now take ya ho'! That's how you met her ass ain't it, naked?" she slammed the door.

Dad yells through the door, "This some dumb ass shit you did Donna. I'm gonna get ya ass for this shit. Fucking Bitch! All out in the street with this bullshit. It ain't even like that. How you gone put house business in the street like that?"

He then turned to Candi and said as he tried to cover

her with his jacket and led her towards the car, "What the fuck you doing coming to my house. I told you that bitch was crazy. You trying to get both of us killed? Come on. What the hell am I supposed to do now? Y'all must come with a gene that doesn't let y'all follow directions."

We sat in Mom's room crying as we looked out of the window, watching Dad pull off... with Candi. We listened to Mom rant and rave in tears to Aunt Jo about Dad. Later that night she set Candi's clothes on fire in the back yard. The next day she pawned the ring and treated herself to something nice.

A few days later, after work Dad came home to get his things, they argued about Candi and Dad's extra marital doings, and then you know they started fighting. Mom stabbed Dad in the leg with a kitchen knife; she had a habit of stashing weapons around the house when they were at it. She was a bit too light in the ass to try to fight him fair. He commenced to kicking her ass after she poked him.

Quintin told me to stay in the room, while he went downstairs. He tried to pull on Dad and make him stop but he kept hitting and kicking Mom. She was fighting back but she was no match for him. Dad was enraged and threw Quintin into a wall while Quintin was trying to get between him and Mom. Quintin hit his head rather hard on the wall and fell to the ground. Mom rushed to Quintin's side to cradle him in her arms and rock him. Realizing that things had gone too far, Dad backed up and stopped fighting Mom. He gave her a dirty look and reached into his pockets. He took a handful of money out and threw it at her as he headed for the door.

As he left he stared my mother down and said, "Fuck you bitch. It didn't have to be like this. All the shit I've done for you. Bitch you wasn't shit. Over nothing, nothing Donna. Well go on ahead bitch, you ain't shit without me. That was the last time we saw him for about five or six years, and even that next meeting was in passing.

After about six months of depression from the break up, or break out, and not hearing from Dad, Mom started to go out again. I think that it really disturbed her that Dad didn't keep in contact, if for no other reason, us. They had been together for over ten years and he just stepped off and didn't look back. I'm sure that made her feel like shit, even though his actions caused the turmoil. She told us over and over again that it's not our fault. She tried to help us understand that Dad's not calling or coming to see us was his way of going through it. This speech ended with "He'll be back. Your Daddy loves y'all, you know that don't you?" She always ended the conversation with these words. But, he never did come back.

Mom started hooking up with some wanna be cool in the game dude named Mook. He was a hustler, of sorts, and they hung out in exciting places, I guess. Look I don't know what the allure was; I think he was just the first to be able to fill the void she had. He was just about her height and asphalt black. He kept his hair cut rather short and was always wearing this P.I.M.P. hat with a feather in it. She started having the red light parties again, but they just seemed slightly out of control now. The element that was hanging at the house wasn't friendly and contained, like when Dad was there. Her friend seemed to be in charge; he and his buddies were taking over. It wasn't their house so they didn't care if they made a mess. Fuck it, Donna will clean up.

Mom started snorting coke, drinking, and hanging out every week. The drugs were always present at the card parties; it's just that Mom wasn't the one getting high. She smoked 'killa' but we'd never known her to do coke or pop pills. Dad used to snort socially, if there is such a thing, and smoke a little 'killa'. We didn't like the guy, Mook, but he seemed to make Mom happy or high or both, and she had-n't been happy in months. If getting high and drunk every weekend was fun, I guess she was having a ball. Over the course of a year her habit got worse and we started to see things fall apart. We seemed to be spending a lot of time with Aunt Jo lately. She and Mom were fallen out.

Aunt Jo says to mom, "Donna, you need to check ya self. You gonna let ya life fall apart because that nigga left. Look at all of the shit y'all was going through. This ain't the first young twat he done had, so why this one matter so much." Mom responded, "Look Jo this is my life. I ain't been happy since he left and now I am. Why you trying to crash my party. I got this. I'm handling my business. Mook treats me good." Aunt Jo replied, "You done up and moved some nigga in the house with ya kids that you barely know, what kind of shit is that. They had been around their dad all they life, now all of a sudden you going through something and you move some new man in. Did you even think about how they feel? Look at you, trippin. You getting high all the time, and got all types of mu'fuckas around them like its cool. It's not. You ain't never messed with coke, now you and Mook, what kind of fucking name is that, now you and him like Scarface and the Quaalude bitch. Ya shit ain't right. You gonna fuck up every-thing you got so you can hold on to some man, that if he really gave a shit about you, he'd have you laying up some-where other than at your house with your kids. That shit ain't cute."

My mom was becoming annoyed and defensive as she sighed and said, "Look Jo, they know that their father ain't shit, I ain't got to tell them that. They need a man around, and Mook ain't doing nothing to them. Don't you think they'd tell me. This is my shit and if you don't like it, you ain't got to be a part of it. I'm grown. I've been taking care of myself a long time. I don't need you telling me how to run my life."

Almost defeated, Aunt Jo responded, "You right. You right. I'll stay out of it. It's your life, you go right ahead and fuck it up. But something happen to one of them kids, I'ma kill ya ass. You hear me? You better check out what your doin."

Quintin never told anyone about the incident I am about to speak of until we were older, when it didn't seem to matter anymore. He woke up one night and had to go to the bathroom. As he walked through the dark hallway, he saw a slither of light coming from Mom's room. He peeked through the crack between the door and the pane, following the harsh smell in the hall and saw Mom and Mook in a smoky room sitting on the bed with the TV on. He saw her snorting coke off the back of her hand and giggling. Mook was sitting next to her lighting a straight shooter, smoking coke. Quintin was frozen, staring through the crack of the door and the room in the darkness. He saw Mook pass the pipe to Mom, saying "come on, try it. It's cool". As he passed the pipe to her everything seemed to be moving in slow motion, almost like that was his queue to run in there and bring everything to a halt, you know his opportunity to change the future. Mom took hold of the reloaded pipe and raised it to her mouth. He lit it for her and she took a deep pull. As she released the smoke, coughing, and laughing, a bright white light seemed to overcome Quintin, drowning him out.

Mom's growing drug habit seemed to just change Quintin after that day. He was cold and blamed Dad for what was happening to Mom. He used to sit downstairs on the living room couch staring out the window waiting for Dad.

Quintin even had a birthday party, Dad had never missed one of Quintin's birthdays, even if he missed whatever festivities were being held. After the party was over he stayed downstairs at the window all night. Dad never showed: I tried to get him to come to bed when it started to get late, but he wouldn't. I heard him crying in the window from the top of the steps. Quintin stayed up all night long waiting and Dad never came or called. Quintin was still in the window when Mom and I got up for breakfast the next morning. It was a sad sight to see him a sleep, hanging off of the back of the couch. Mom was upset that Quintin was upset, and went on a raving coke binge after she cooked us a good ole family breakfast and sent us to school. Quintin never said anymore about Dad after that day and never expected him to come through again. See, I don't know if it really was Dad's fault that all this shit jumped off, but I know that the things he's doing or rather not doing aren't helping.

By the time the next school year started Mom had lost her job, which she had been at for 10 years, and the mortgage was so backed up that they were about to foreclose on the house. My mom had officially become a "CRACK-HEAD". We couldn't believe what had happened over the course of a year. My Mom and Mook broke up when her habit was taking all the money and she couldn't buy him a hit anymore. This was actually a good thing. I think. It seems that when Quintin and I returned from our visits with Aunt Jo, Mom was battered and bruised a lot. She said that Mook wasn't hittin on her but we weren't stupid and knew otherwise. I stopped talking or caring as much, started keeping to myself and just worrying about school and my dolls. Quintin seemed to always be in a fight. He hadn't totally lost his mind, he wouldn't fight in, or on school grounds. If Mom had to come up to the school for some bullshit, it was curtains. Aunt Jo tried to explain to us that Mom was going through some changes and wasn't thinking clearly. The way she explained it, it was easier to just rationalize that she was not really being herself than to believe that she was as fucked up as she was.

Mom told us we were going to have to move. Unemployment and welfare couldn't feed us and pay the bills anymore. Pay for her habit is more like it. November 1st we packed up what was left to take from the house into a U-Haul and moved to Tasker Projects, 422B. It was two bedrooms, one bath and nasty. Mom and I each had a room, Quintin slept downstairs in the living room on a pull out couch. I cried myself to sleep for a month. It was all so depressing, like a bad dream. I would go to sleep every night praying that when I woke up and my mother would be back.

Mom took us to get enrolled in school one morning. All of the neighborhood kids were leaving for school, all of them grittin hard. We knew we were new victims, fresh meat. First of all, Quintin, had mentally attempted to take over the role as the head of the household. Mind you he was about 12, had no job, or pull with our mom. Having our father always there and then suddenly gone left him hollow. At the time he was unable to communicate his emotions, but he couldn't fathom how a man that takes on the responsibilities of a wife, children, career... everything as far as we were concerned and just let it all go and never turn back. Quintin blamed himself, not necessarily for my father leaving but in some bizarro world plane he felt that somehow he was supposed to be able to make him come back. My father and Quintin had a bond, shit he was his first born son, that's supposed to hold water, but after he and my mom had this last fight, it didn't seem to have the weight Quintin thought it did.

In Quintin's mind, he was dead, and even if he wasn't, he should have been.Quintin got chased home by a bunch of boys from the projects. He dipped on them. Quintin ain't no fool, he had mapped out a route home the day before, and just made it. This shit went on for a while, like a week or two, and then they caught him. Some boys named

Ace, Fido, Clent and their squad. All of them was nasty, grimy little troublemakers. Ace looked like he could have been Hispanic or something of an exotic nature. He had cropped curls about his head and olive colored skin. Now Fido was ashy, black and dirty looking. According to my new girl-friends, he stayed picking a fight with someone. Clent on the other hand was cute and yellow like Pikachu, with big ears. He basically just hung along. I think that was because he was the biggest in weight, they used him for muscle. Anyhow, they were fucking Quintin up pretty good.

My mom was already worried when she was on her way across the projects to knock on doors. On her way, around the corner from one of the buildings, she saw a group of guys in a circle making a lot of noise. Now in case you don't know already, my brother was in the midst of this gang getting his ass handed to him something awful. So my mom, crackhead, crazy bitch that she is, grabbed a pole, which in the projects wouldn't be hard to come across, and headed toward the crowd ready for war.

She just started to swing the pole. She hit whoever was there and keeping her from getting to Quintin. Now we aren't talking respectful kids, for the most part, so after drop-ping four or five young men to their knees, someone sucker-punched her. So now the picture changes. You got my broth-er being stomped and punched, my mom runs up smacking niggas with a pole and now she and my brother are getting rolled on.

Luckily everyone in the projects is not all fucked up and a few adults came out of their residents to stop the com-motion. Four or five men, some related to the gang members in participation came out and broke up the fight. Mom and Quintin limped home all beat the fuck up, dirty and tired. They actually weren't that battered, but damn I know that was a workout.

So... my mom and Quintin get home. Quintin runs up to the bathroom to wash his wounds, closes himself in and cries. He didn't have his own room, so we just had to bear with him. I tried to check on him, but he told me to "fuck off." He was hurt. His pride was hurt and his manhood, he felt was diminished. So this begins the birth of a bad ass.

Quintin acted like he didn't even hear mom bitchin' like she was and headed upstairs to the bathroom. Mom kept right on flippin' out. As I headed up the stairs to see how Quintin really was, he heard me coming up the stairs and locked the bathroom door.

Quintin knew that my mother's help would only assist him in more frequent or brutal ass whippings, that's just how it is. You don't get revered for your ballsy mother who came out and 'got it in' with you. You get berated for being a punk, despite the masses, for your mother having to come save your ass.

So the next day after school, Quintin did what he did the day before. He got out of class, gathered his shit as fast as he could and got to running home. And like the day before, the boys were on him and caught him. This time instead of trying to drop his stuff and fight, he waited. He let the first guy, the leader come up to him and start talking shit while he stood there, meek, timid and quiet. The guy got up in his face and was talking shit to him.

The boy, said, "You a fucking bitch ass nigga. Fucking mom had to come help ya ass. I don't see ya fucking mom today though bitch (mugs him). Now what, you gone cry pussy boy? Huh?"

This kid, later to be determined as Ace, punched Quintin in the face. Quintin fell back onto the ground and reached inside the book bag that he was holding for dear life. He pulled my mom's biggest kitchen knife out of it and hid it along side his arm. He came up from the ground without the book bag and without the knife being visible. He stood right where he was the first time the kid hit him. Again the boy Ace said, "Oh, you got some heart, huh? Well I want to see you go down again."

Ace went to hit Quintin and Quintin grabbed his arm and spun him around so that his back was to Quintin while Quintin held him close with the knife to his throat. The boy was facing the rest of the mob. Ace was scared to death. The other kids were scared to death. Quintin was scared to death. Think "The Good, the Bad & the Ugly" when Clint Eastwood is in the triangle standoff.

Quintin yells as he eyes all of the boys, "Look y'all mu'fuckas ain't gone be chasing me home every fucking day. Y'all ain't gonna be rolling on me every fucking day. I don't know which one of y'all hit my mom but I'ma cut all y'all fucking bitches throats you keep fucking with me. Now what? Move, I fucking dare you. I'll cut him the fuck up. Y'all a bunch of punks. Don't nobody want a fair one, huh, how' bout now. Want a fair one now?" One of the kids pleads, "Let him go, man. It ain't that major."

Quintin yells back, "No, I ain't letting him go. Fuck you. Go get my mom and I'll let him go. Other than that his ass will be walking me home just the fuck like this or dragged and bleeding. Sick of y'all bitches."
Ace cries, "Come on man, damn we was just playin' around. Let me go." Quintin yells as he nudges Ace from behind, "Shut up. Bitch ass, now you scared. Fuck you."

A few of the boys ran off to get Ace's mom and our mom. Quintin wasn't bullshitting; he wasn't letting him go and had not let him go by the time my mother walked up... after Ace's mom had arrived. When my mom got there, Ace's mom was pleading with Quintin to let him go. Quintin told her no, not disrespectfully, but he told her no. So then my mom walks up. There was a moment of familiarity and then one of clarity as both parents realized where they had seen one another before. They were on crack; they had seen each other on one of their important, unmissable crack conferences. After a few moments of reliving the good times, Mom having a way about herself, stopped all this shit real quick.

My mom says, "Quintin, put my fucking good knife down and let that boy go. Now!" Quintin snaps, "I ain't going through this shit everyday."

Sternly my mom says, "You cursing at me?" Quintin replies, "I'm sorry mom. I ain't gonna be running from nobody everyday. I'll kill him first, I ain't runnin, I ain't no punk."

My mother makes an attempt to reason with him and says, "Look now, this shit is over baby. Let him go, they ain't gonna fuck with you no more. Let him go, come on. Let him go before the police decide to actually do their job, come on. Baby, come on. Let's go home, let him go."

Quintin let the boy go. He and mom walked home together and Ace with his mother. I was in the living room watching TV when they came back.

As they entered the house I said, "Yo Mike Tyson, Don King promoting for you again."

Quintin gave me the finger on his way up to my room and mom went in her room, preparing to go back out. After a few minutes mom left, then a young boy came to the house. I heard a knock at the door and answered it. I opened the door slowly and said hello. I was not at all alarmed to see a dirty faced, dirty clothed little boy with snot coming out of his nose asking for "Quitman." I stared for a moment and without taking my eyes off the boy I yelled up the stairs to Quintin. "Some boy is here for you."

I shook my head and slammed the door in the little boys face. Dumb shit, glad I ain't got balls. See this degrading, negroidian, gladiator like manner of problem solving called for a real asshole, a real man to back his boy, a dick like my Dad. But hey, in absentia...

It was a quiet talk I'll tell you that. I knew better than to say anything and I think Quintin was pondering over all of the things I was thinking. What had occurred was that both mothers made the boys shake and make up. Mom and Ace's mom had gone to get high, celebrating a victory and a loss, I guess. Who the fuck knows the thought processes of a crackhead. After that episode mom and Ace's mom started to hang the same with Quintin and Ace. I think that the get high factor had something to do with it. That shit kills the pre-fight dozens quick:

"Ya mom is a crackhead!

Oh yeah, well ya mom is a ..... OH!"

That evening, late at night, Quintin came to my bedroom. He crept in and sat on the bed next to me. He was crying, I could hear him sniffling in the dark as I woke and got myself together. He didn't say anything until he heard me speak first as I whispered," Quintin? What's wrong?" Sniffling, he answered softly, "Nothing. Nothing." As I moved to make room for him, I invited him, "Get up here with me." He answered quietly, "Naw." There was a pause, "You know I would have cut him." Puzzled I said, "Huh?"

To clarify what he was talking about he said, "Ace, today, I would have cut him if I had to, and it really didn't bother me earlier, I was scared and shit, but I'm thinking back and I would have and I don't think I cared either. What does that mean? Something ain't right Sis; I ain't ever been that mad before, I ain't never just known, you know. When I got robbed that time before we moved, I was scared and I acted without thinking, but I wasn't angry. Today, I was so angry when I grabbed him by the neck, I wanted somebody to move wrong so I could cut him, and I wanted to cut him.

Am I crazy?"

I hugged him to try to calm him but I couldn't explain and didn't know why he was feeling like he did. I thought he was crazy all his life, but hey what do I know at 11.

Almost crying, I tried to console him, "Quintin, don't cry, it's gonna be OK. You were just afraid. You did what you had to; they were gonna fuck you up. You ain't crazy; you just know how to survive. Stop crying. Come on now, you gonna make me cry. You ain't no punk, is all." I start to sniffle and we both lied there, holding one another, consoling, until we fell asleep.

Quintin started playing basketball for a neighborhood league. He had sprouted over the summer and seemed destined to be tall as, or if not taller than our dad. He was really good at basketball and his height helped. This was the last year of Junior High School. He was good, he even got better and better over time; this also. gave him something to do instead of getting into trouble. He needed decent grades in order to play and he made sure he got them. It gave him something to hope for, something to look forward to; that and my mom would have killed him, crackhead or not, if his grades weren't up to par. In his mind I think he believed that basketball and fame would be his way of getting back at our dad.

During the same year, Ace's cousin Duane put Ace and Quintin on to dealing drugs while in Junior High School. Duane would let the boys hang out with him on the weekends and Ace was with him almost everyday after school. Since Quintin had basketball practice and games to worry about, he wasn't able to hang full time. Duane would pay the boys to cap up the crack for him at some nasty crackhead's house, on the weekends. He'd pay them $50 and hour to cap up and would feed them lunch, dinner, or whatever meal they were working through. See, to Quintin this was his hustle, his way to help provide for the family. He had bogarted the roll of head of household and was seemingly serious about it. I mean considering our father was like the out of the family, I guess that's what the oldest son does.

Quintin continued selling drugs by night and going to school, playing the All-star, by day. One day there was a big tournament game at the school. Quintin had taken a dime of herb to school to smoke after the game against their rivals. He had a small .22 caliber in the pocket of his backpack from his previous night's shift on the streets. He became accustom to carrying a weapon. As they were leaving and making preparations for partying the night away, drama started. Quintin was walking home with some of the cheerleaders and a few of his teammates along with some fans just joining in the celebration. Some spectators from the other school pulled up in a truck and started a fight with Quintin and his teammates. It turned into a big mess. Quint, Ace, Somaat, a guy they had just started rolling with from school, the team and half of the neighborhood was fighting. By the time the cops came, there were just groups of people fighting in different areas of the park. When they caught up with Quint, he didn't realize he still had herb in his pocket or the gun in his backpack. They hemmed him up and found his stash, and the gun, Quintin was up shits creek. He just knew Mom was going to kill him.

The police did charge him with the gun, but not the weed and trust me you could see the wheels turning as they cuffed him. He was thinking of a lie, a lie that would get his ass released without the bail. Well that didn't happen. Mom didn't have the money to post bail Bottom line was that he couldn't play ball anymore. Under the agreement for the school to request leniency and probation, Quintin's career was officially over. Proverbial rock and hard place.

Duane at some point near to this, started to encourage Ace and Quintin to sell bundles (pre-packaged dollar amounts of drugs) and hitting the corners to make some 'real' money. I mean isn't $50, an hour, real money to a kid, broke in the ghetto. He would tell them the basics about looking out for stick up kids, cops and scamming crackheads that don't take no for an answer in search of credit or free-bees. He'd also urge them not to fuck up in school. He'd slide them a little cash each week to help ensure his demands. All he wanted was his money off the bundle.

Ok, so the first time Quintin gets a bundle, who does he tell but me, like I know or care what it all means. He was excited, but had a look of fear and uncertainty in his eyes when he approached me. So he comes running into my room around 11:30pm one night. His eyes are all big and crazy looking. So I'm thinking that something has happened to him or something.So I say, "What's wrong? What's wrong?!" Quintin hastily responded by, "Shhhh! Mommy here?" Inquisitive now, I say, "No, what's wrong?"He answers, "Look."

He reaches under his pullover Raiders jacket and pulls out a brown paper bag that's kinda shaped like a ball. He opens the bag and pours out umpteen little vials of what looks like whitish yellow rocks, then he stares at me like I should have something to say so I come up with, "What the heck is that?"

Quintin informs me, "That's crack. I'm selling it."So I say, "What? Crack? You selling crack. Mommy gonna kick ya butt when she find out."Again shushing me he said, "Shut up. You better not tell her then. Somebody gotta bring some money up in here. You see the electric bill? They getting ready to cut shit off in here. "Defensive of my mother's char-acter I say "Nah un. Mommy wouldn't let 'em turn off the heat and stuff."

With extreme sarcasm he says, "This your first day?

Like I said, they getting ready to turn shit off. She ain't paying no bills man. Are you serious, shit half the time she don't even open them up." Thinking over whether or not what he just said held any truth to it I say, "Quintin, you can't be a drug dealer. What if something happens to you? What if you get arrested?"

Quintin sees that all of this has begun to upset me. He sits down on the bed and with his hands between his legs and with his head down he sighs.

In an attempt to justify the career choice he's elected he says, "I love you and ain't nobody here to take care of us right now but us. This ain't really what I think MJ did on his way to stardom but shit we still got to eat. You can't tell anyone, I mean nobody Sis, about this but if ain't nobody else to do it, then I got to take care of you. I'm the only male of the house now so I got to be the man of the house.

That night while out hustling on his shift, a guy was approaching Quintin while he was alone. Now Quintin is scared, but he's not really sure if the guy is a crackhead, stick up kid, or the police. So his heart is racing, his hands are sweating and he's so fucking scared he can't move his legs. He holds the gun that Duane advised him to carry under his Raiders pull over jacket and removes the safety. He doesn't know what the hell he's gonna do, should he run, should he start bussing, what? Duane had not briefed him for this particular situation. As he approaches Quintin the guy yells, "Hey youngboy, you holdin'?" Apprehensively Quintin answers, "Huh?"

Slightly more aggressive the man says, "I said you holding? Let me get 4 for $10." Again Quintin replies in the same tone, "Huh?" Pissed off now, the guy says, "Look you little bitch, you heard me. I said give me…"

The guy began to reach in his jacket. Quintin didn't know what was going to happen. He was shaking, he closed his eyes pulled out the gun and started to shoot. He shot the gun three times. When he opened his eyes he saw the guy falling to the ground and the headlights of the man's car at the corner were on. They were headed his way. The gun was hot to touch and Quintin was scared, so scared he had pissed on himself. He saw the lights coming and turned and ran the other direction. He cut through a lot where they had demolished a row home and just kept running. As the car sped at him, the inhabitants had started to shoot at him and from the sounds of it, whatever they were carrying was bigger than that shit he had. He ran and ran. He stopped to catch his breath a couple of blocks away. He was bent over and shaking when he looked up. He realized where he was and headed down the alley. He was by a club called the "Back Cave". Duane had bought him and Ace by here a few times. He went to the door in the alley and banged and banged. Yelling for help Quintin says, "Open the door. Help. Help. Open the fucking door, please. PLEASE."

The door swung open after a few moments and in the doorway was a man emitting the aura of an O.G. aiming a sawed off shot gun at Quintin's head. Quintin stood frozen with his eyes like a deer in headlights. The man, Skow, initiates conversation in a raspy voice, "What the fuck you banging on my god-damned door for?" Still frightened Quintin mumbles, "Hi sir. I'm a friend of Ace's, Duane's little cousin. Please help me. Please. I need help."

Quintin still had the gun in his hand and was attempting to hand it over to Skow, the tall, lanky, balding owner of the bar. He had a cigar hanging from the corner of his mouth. Skow, said while looking around, "Get in here. You look like sin dipped in misery."

Skow shut the door after he invited Quintin in. He told Quintin to have a seat on the couch in his office while he locked the door leading to the club.

Reeking of embarrassment and shaking his head in despair, Quintin answered, "I can't, sir." With one eyebrow raised, Skow asked, "Ya knees bend don't they?"Again with his head down Quintin answered, "No, I mean yes sir, but I don't want to mess up you stuff." (He looked down at the moisture on his pants)With his eyebrow still raised, slightly more now, Skow said, "What?"

Skow walked over to Quintin and looked him up and down. He too could now see the stream of moisture down Quintin's pants. He laughed he tapped his cigar ash to the floor. Reassuring himself that the door was locked, Skow says, "You done been in some deep shit, made you piss on ya self. Take them pants off; I got some sweats around here somewhere. Let me get you something to put on. So what happened?"

Skow was looking around the office for something for Quintin to change into. Quintin was too nervous to start talking about what had transpired while he was moving around the room. Unwillingly Quintin mumbled, "Well..." With authority Skow urges him, "Look boy, can't nobody help you if you don't say what's wrong. So what the fuck is wrong. You knew to come here, so come on now, coochie don't stay wet forever. "With the joke well over his head Quintin starts his story, "Well sir, I was" As he stopped in his tracks, he turned to Quintin and said, "You call me sir one more fucking time and I'ma shoot you."

Now alarmed Quintin started again, "Sorry s-, sorry. I was on the block and this guy came up and I had the gun and I got scared and I , I , I closed my eyes and shot. Then this car was coming at me and the guy was on the ground and they was shooting at me and, and I ran."

Quintin was in tears, he was shaking and terrified. Skow poured him a shot of something brown from the mini bar and handed it to him and said with encouragement,

"Here suck that down, it'll help."

Quintin threw back the shot and damn near choked to death. This made Skow laugh again. He came over to Quintin and patted him on the head and sat next to him on the couch.

Taking a deep breath and trying to exude a hint of paternal nurturing, Skow says, with a sigh, "So I take it that's the first time you shot a gun?"

Quickly, Quintin responds, "No s-, no." Tossing his head whimsically, Skow says, "OK, so that was the first time you shot somebody?" Quintin says, "Yes."

Nodding as he pondered his next question, Skow asks, "You think he's dead?" Quintin shrugs his shoulders. Skow asks, "You want him to be dead?"

Quintin shrugs his shoulders.

Skow then asked, "Where'd this happen? You think he's still out there?" Quintin readily told him, "He was on the ground when I came here."

Skow took the gun from Quintin. He got up and stepped out of the office into the club and then returned with some other man when he said, "You stay here. I'll be right back, OK? Y'all young boys want in the game, but y'all all from Missouri; y'all don't believe fat meat greasy. "Unsure of what that meant, Quintin replied, "Yes?"

Skow and the man left out the back door. Quintin sat there and waited. Skow and the other man had gone back to the block where Quintin was selling drugs. They went to see if there was a body lying out there or perhaps the police. When they rode through, Skow noticed some blood on the ground, but there was no one out there. NO POLICE. They came back. As he poured a shot and with a head gesture offered Quintin another round he said, "Well you didn't kill him. OK, well he ain't on the ground no more and I didn't see any police. Let me take you home, it's late somebody gonna be looking for you soon."

Skow drove Quintin home in silence, when they pulled up in front of Quintin's house the car stopped. Quintin opened the door and started to get out of the car. He was interrupted when Skow said, "I want you to come by my club after school. And don't worry about what happened, it's all in the game, son. This is a part of hustling, so I guess you got some stuff to think about, huh. Is the money worth what you gonna have to do sometimes to get it? Think about it."

Grateful to be alive and home Quintin said, "Thank you, for everything. I didn't mean to bring no trouble to you." Skow smiled and nodded, "Don't worry about it, you just come by tomorrow. You and ... what's his name, Duane's little cuz." Helpfully supplying the information, Quintin uttered, "Ace?" While nodding Skow said, "Yeah, you and Ace come by after school."

So from this point, Skow became the father figure that Quintin was missing. He was there for him, when he needed help, and was trying to mold him to be an upstanding dope dealer. Skow would become the person Quintin sought for insight, advice and to tell of the many firsts' he and Ace were to encounter as new entries into The Game.

Nikia Comfort Born in Voorhees, NJ and raised in South Philly/South Jersey and even a stint in West Africa. Nikia has just completed her first play write/book entitled "Taming the Phoenix", and is hard at work on her second work entitled "The Truth About Men & Women". Nikia@whosnextentertainment.com. Nikia is a favorite in spoken word arenas throughout the Phila. NJ and DE area. Her CD entitled 'Failing to Tame the Phoenix' will be released in June of 2005.

Seventeen

Kimberly Smith

Maxine Davis stood 5"5 130lbs, chestnut brown complexion, long straight hair, almond shaped eyes. Maxine's smile was to die for. She was only 16 but she was very curvaceous, kind of like a long neck coca cola bottle. She got much attention for her looks; she was a normal teenager with not much experience with boys.

Maxine entered her junior year at Kennedy High School in the Bronx this fall. She was on the cheerleading squad and she definitely got compliments on the way she looked in her uniform. Kennedy Knights were playing against Clinton High on this particular day in a basketball game.

"Give me a V-I-C-T-O-R-Y, give me a V-I-C-T-O-R-Y...,"the squad chanted as Kennedy beat Clinton 65-47.The opponents' side was booing the Knights, throwing things at the players and cheerleaders.

Normally, the girls would get rides with the coach but today Maxine and her friends decided to take the bus home. As Maxine and her girls, Stacey and Liz, were waiting for the bus, talking about the beating that the Knights gave Clinton, a car pulled up with three guys wearing Clinton jackets. Two guys jumped out of the car and started harassing the girls. The driver of the car shouted, "Come on, let's go!" The other boys ignored his pleads. He drove off.

One of the boys pointed at Maxine and said that's her. He yanked on Maxine skirt causing it to rip. "What are you doing? Get off of me!" Maxine said. "Who you think you talking to shorty? The guy said." "Listen why don't you leave us alone" Liz said.

An older man walked up to the bus stop and noticed that the boys were harassing the girls. "You boys need to go on with that! Have some respect for those girls, they could be your, sisters or girlfriends." "Old man you need to mind your business" Troy said. The old man looked at Troy and said "You should be a shame of yourself" and walked away.

The girls began to walk away. "I don't think so girls" The other guy grabbed Maxine. "Let her go! Let her go! Stacey shouted. Liz grabbed the boy who was doing all the talking. "Why the hell are you Clinton dudes tripping?" "Akeem tell them why we mad son" Akeem began calling the girls names. "Tramps, Hoes, Sluts!" Troy interrupted, "You Kennedy bitches make us sick, always jumping around in those little uniforms. Showing off your asses." "So now, we want to see how much you can shout and jump around now. "We are here to give you what you want, a VICTORY," said Troy.

Just then the old man appeared with a young man holding a stick, he had a coco complexion, was about six feet, with sexy hazel eyes, he was slim but had a muscular body, you could see the cuts through his t-shirt. "What seems to be the problem ladies?" the young guy said. "These guys are in our way" Liz screamed. "Fellas I think you should be going now." "If we don't?" Troy said boldly "Well then I'm going to have to use my stick here and you won't like what my friends in the gym are holding" the young guy said. Troy and Akeem smiled at the girls as they walk away. "See you at the next game shorty" Akeem whispered.

Stacey was overwhelmed with gratitude "Thank you so much! Thank you!!!" Liz said, "Good thing you came when you did. Who knows what would have happened."

"My name is Bryan, and this here is..." the young guy hesitated. "Mr. Owens, I'm Mr. Owens" the old man said. I couldn't just leave you girls like that, knowing those were a bunch of knuckle heads. I saw a group of guys going into the gym and this fine young man gave me a hand."

"Well thank you both so much, Mr. Owens" Maxine said. "My name is Maxine. These are my girls, Stacey and Liz." "Great game the Knights had. You girls did your thing with those cheers." Bryan said. "Yeah we gave them a hurting. Well we have to go thanks again," said Maxine. As the girls headed off Mr. Owens yelled out "You girls be safe." Bryan on the other hand couldn't believe he just helped out the girl who he had a secret crush on. He would watch Maxine all the time at the games. He thought to his self, "She's going to be mine."

"That was pretty scary. Max, are you ok?" Stacey blurted. "Yeah I'm ok, it was kind of bugged out" Maxine said. Girl you seen honey's eyes! He is gorgeous, did you notice those deep delicious dimples." Liz said. "Did I! He was scrumptious," Maxine said.

Liz and Stacey were Maxine's only real friends. Max met Liz in kindergarten they had been best friends ever since. Liz was about five feet, weighing in at 150lbs, She is what we called big boned, she was half black and Puerto Rican so she had that butter-pecan complexion, she had curly hair. She was the more out spoken one; never bit her tongue for no one. She reminded me of a little Rosy Perez from "Do the Right Thing".

Liz and Max meet Stacey in Junior High School, they needed one more girl to make the squad complete so they grabbed the first girl they saw. Not knowing it but Liz and Max were the only friends Stacey had made in JHS.

Stacey has a mahogany glow that complemented her brown complexion. Stacey is very tall, and weighs, 125lbs. She has the straightest white teeth I ever seen on anyone. She has beautiful dark brown eyes but they were hidden behind her black pointy glasses that she had ever since JHS. She wore a pony tail all the time, just think we were in high school and Stacey was still sporting a pony tail. Stacey was the rational thinker in the group she always thought things out before she did them.

Maxine on the other hand was the dreamer of the crew, she's always dreaming. Her biggest dream is to leave NY and go far away to college to study law and never return. She wanted so bad to see the good in everyone. Most of her dreams brought out the craziest ideas. Those ideas would land the girls in detention and on punishment. One time back in Junior High School Maxine thought of a way to make money to get to the cheerleading competition in Maryland. She decided that they could sale things to the girls in school like lotions, maxi pads, and perfumes things like that. Well when the principal found out that they were charging students, a call went out to each of their parents.

Maxine had to stop by Liz' house to change into a

different outfit. If she walked in her house and her father saw that uniform ripped and she had to tell the story of the day's events, off of the squad she would be. Maxine lived with her father David and Brother Mike. David was a middle-aged man with touches of gray scatter through his hair and mustache, he was still muscular for his age, he had this scary deep voice that would intimidate everyone that came by or called the house. Her brother Mike who was 3 years older than her, had the same features his father had but he was a younger version so everything seemed to stand out more, he had a smooth caramel complexion, bushy eye-brows, he had that same to die for smile that his little sister had, he didn't have much of the facial hair that his father had, he styled a Caesar, and had a nice body, all of Maxine's friends had a crush on him.

Maxine's mom passed away sixteen years ago during labor with Maxine, She only knows things that people tell her about her mother. "Oh you look just like your momma girl" or the favorite from her Aunt V "Marie was a big dreamer, just like you. She wanted to move far away from NY too. But she fell in love with your dad."

Aunt V was a big help in her life. Aunt V whose name is Vanessa is her mom little sister, she helped David out with Maxine after her sister passed, she would help with her hair, dressing her, she even spoke to her about her menstruation and sex, and other girly-girl issues that a man may not have had the answers to.

It was because of Aunt V that she was able to join the cheerleading team that her dad was so against. Maxine thought back to the day her Aunt V convinced her Dad to sign her consent form. David, now why can't the girl join the squad? Don't you trust her to know right from wrong?" "V it isn't that, I just don't want my girl thrown to the wolves." stated David. "David, trust her to do the right things, you taught her well." Aunt V said.

Maxine was relieved that she changed her clothes at Liz' house. As she was walking into her building she ran into her Dad. That night, Maxine got down on her knees to say a prayer "Dear God, Thank you for helping me out today, you are always with me and you chose the best person to be my guardian angel, my mom. I ask that you bless Mr. Owens for standing up for us and Bryan for stopping those boys. I ask that you bless us all…Amen." Maxine laid on her queen size canopy bed and stared into the air, she saw the face of Bryan and thought, "wasn't he just so fine". "I wonder if he has a girlfriend, I'm to young for him anyway" Maxine thought. Maxine went to sleep, she usually dreams about graduation day but tonight she had sweet dreams about Bryan.

The next morning, Liz met Maxine at her house. "What's up girl? Maxine I hope you don't mind but I asked my sister Angela to give us a ride to school today, I called Stacey. She said she'll meet up with us at school. Maxine got through her math class but by the time she began social studies class she wasn't feeling to well. Mr. Weiss spoke, "Ms. Davis can you please tell me what invention Garret Morgan invented?" Ms. Davis. Maxine was daydreaming and didn't hear her teacher Mr. Weiss calling her name. "Excuse me" whispered Maxine. A girl from the back then yelled out "Garret Morgan invented the traffic light." Maxine turned around and rolled her eyes at the mousy looking girl. "Can I have the bathroom pass Sir?"

As Maxine began to walk down the hall to Liz' class someone grabbed her from behind. It was Lance, the star basketball player Lance was about 5'9, light-skin with corn-rows, he was kind of slinky not very muscular but he was very attractive. He was what we called a pretty boy. He had a sense of humor that drove the girls crazy. But guess which girl got his attention back in freshmen year.

Max and Lance dated for half of the semester. They made the perfect match because he was on the basketball team and she was on the cheerleading squad. They got to spend a lot of time together until her Daddy found out about it. Her father thought she was too young and that she should at least wait until she turned seventeen to have a boyfriend. So Max ended it with Lance. Lance still adore her, they remained good friends.

"Maxine I'm waiting on you, when are you going to become my girl again and marry me?" Lance joked. Lance always seemed to make Max blush. "Your smile gets my juices flowing. When I'm out on the court and I see you doing your routines, you inspire me to take it to the hole," said Lance. "Lance you are a mess. So when you make it to the Pros and get the "Rookie of the Year" award be sure to let the world know it was all because of Maxine Davis. Lance you know you will always be my first love." Maxine said. "Just say the word girl." said Lance. He kissed Max on the forehead and left.

Just one more year she thought and out of New York and on my own in college. "What's up Lance?" Stacey said as she walked up to Max. "B-Ball girl!" shouted Lance.

"So Max, Are you going to give that boy another chance?" said Stacey. Max was the only one out of the three of them who still was a virgin. Stacey and Liz broke their virginity back in freshmen year. They all were supposed to go along with it but Maxine chickened out at the last minute. Max ignored Stacey's question. "Stacey I'm leaving at lunch, I got cramps"

Max got Liz's attention as she stared hard through the window of her class door. Liz meets Max and Stacey outside the bathroom door. "What's up ladies? Said Stacey. "I'm ready to go I got cramps. I'm leaving my lunch period." Said

Maxine. "Well I have a test sixth period so I got to stay Max but I'll catch up with you at The Plaza." The Plaza was where everyone hung out after school, where girls met up with their boyfriends and made out, there was always music and a lot of skateboarding and dancing. It was right next to the library, so when you told your parents you'd be at the library, you weren't lying.

Fourth period was over and Max and Stacey headed for the number 1 train. As they were walking to the train, a car that looked familiar pulled up beside them. "Hello Maxine," a voice said. As they looked inside, they noticed the face. It was Bryan. "Hi Bryan" said Stacey. "Hey, Which is it Stacey or Liz?" "Stacey! It's Stacey. Hello to you." said Maxine. Maxine thought oh my God this has to be fate. "Do you girls need a ride?" "We are good, thanks" said Stacey. "Come on, the least I can do is give you girls a ride." Bryan knew this was no coincidence. He was over near Kennedy with the intentions of bumping into Maxine. He was feeling her and with her leaving school early, this was his opportunity.

"I know you from somewhere" Stacey said. "Well I've been to all the Knights games. I even play ball in the gym sometimes." Bryan responded. "Yeah maybe that's where I've seen you" said Stacey. Maxine was really quiet because inside she was dying to know if he was trying to kick it to her. "I promise I won't bite. Really I won't hurt you girls." He said slowly batting those bedroom eyes of his and poking his lip out slightly.

Max and Stacey got into the car. Bryan was wearing a navy blue Karl Kani sweatsuit with a pair of white Jordan's. Maxine thought to herself, he looks so good and smells good too he's wearing Calvin Klein Obsession for men. "So where to ladies?" said Bryan. "You can drive us to 161st and the Grand Concourse if you don't mind." said Max. "Isn't school back the other way?" he asked. "Well we left for lunch and since Max isn't feeling well we are going to her Aunt V's house." "Sorry to hear that" he said. When he told Maxine to sit in the front seat her palms began to sweat and her heart was racing because now she knew that he could be feeling her. Why else would he tell her to sit in the front?

"So do you have a man?' Bryan pried. "Who are you asking that?" Maxine asked. "Nope Max doesn't have a man. Do you have a girl?" asked Stacey. "I'm single and looking." said Bryan. Maxine rolled her neck and head toward his direction and asked, "What's with the question?" Taken by her feistiness, Bryan said, "You are a pretty girl, someone I would like to get to know more of. I just wanted to know if you were attached before I made a fool of myself and asked you out."

Stacey was enjoying the show from the back. Max was now blushing and her smile made Bryan's heart skip a beat. "How old are you? He asked. "I'll be seventeen in two weeks." "So what, that makes you a junior?" "Yes I'm a junior. How about you? How old are you?" Maxine couldn't keep still now she was moving in her seat. She began messing with the seat belt. "I'm twenty; I go to Lehman College, as I said earlier I'm single. I just got out of a relationship that I thought was going somewhere but she wasn't looking for the same thing." Maxine and Bryan were so deep in conversation that they forgot about Stacey in the back seat. Until she yelled "Right there the building on your left. "Thanks for the ride" said Stacey. "No problem shorty.

So Maxine can we exchange numbers?" asked Bryan." As they exchanged numbers Max said, "Listen Bryan I can't get calls after ten. My father is really serious about that." "Got it, talk to you soon" said Bryan.

Stacey began teasing Max. "I thought you were about to jump out the car. You were wiggling around like a worm. That brother sure had your panties in a bunch." "Isn't he fly! A college guy, who wants to talk to me," At that moment Maxine felt on top of the world. The girls meet up with Liz and filled her in on this afternoon's happenings. "Liz I'm feeling him, I can't wait until he calls me." Liz said, "Don't you know you don't give a dude your number. You always keep them waiting." Stacey laughed "Girl that's why you're not with Dennis now." "Shut up! Hoe." Liz said jokingly.

The girls hung out at The Plaza for about an hour than went home. Max was getting in the shower when the phone rang. "Maxine telephone!" shouted Mike. Maxine picked up the phone "Hello this is Maxine." "Hi, there Maxine. I've been thinking about you all day." said the voice on the other end. "Bryan, I didn't think you would call." said Max. "That's not the impression I was trying to leave you with. I'm feeling everything about you. When can I take you out?" Bryan asked. "Maxine was excited but yet didn't want to seem easy, so she played a little hard to get. "How do I know you don't say that to all the girls you meet?" "You don't know me but I'll let you know that I'm for real." answered Bryan. Well I'm really flattered but I have plans with my girls this weekend. Maybe we can hook up next week."

"I'm going to have to wait a whole week to see you again. I don't think I can do that. What are you doing now? Can I come over?"

"I was getting in the shower" said Maxine. "So what you got on? Please let me come see you it's not even nine o'clock yet" begged Bryan. "I guess I can meet you in front for half an hour. I live at 1244 West Farms Blvd. Ring 3A when you get here." said Maxine.

Bryan pulled up in front of Max's building. It was a very quiet block. Three buildings and an elementary school is what made the block. There wasn't a lot of traffic or people in the block but on the main street there was a lot of traffic passing by. Maxine was outside waiting "Hey you! Did you find your way ok?" said Maxine as she entered the car. . She was wearing a pair of black sweat pants and a blue Scooby Doo t-shirt that hugged her breast tightly." "I like that T-shirt on you." Bryan caught her off guard as he reached over to give her a kiss. "Someone is very bold" blurted Maxine. Maxine thought to herself "he's a bit aggressive." They sat and talked in the car asking each other questions about their lives. Their likes and dislikes. Maxine lost track of time and she noticed her brother Mike walking over to the car.

"Well I have to go, the warden calls. I'll talk to you later." "Maxine can I see you again? Maybe pick you up from school tomorrow?" asked Bryan. "Sure that will be nice." Mike was trying to see the face in the car but Maxine came out before he could see. "Who's that Max? Maxine rolled her eyes and said "No one here to see you." I got two more weeks until I turn seventeen. Then I don't have to worry about you sneaking up on me when I'm talking to a guy." Maxine ran upstairs to call Stacey and Liz on three-way to tell them what just happened.

The next day Bryan was there to pick up Maxine. They began spending a lot of time together. By the third week they were an item boyfriend and girlfriend. Maxine's Dad wasn't too thrilled but she was seventeen. David set the rules for her. "No late night phone calls, school comes first, no hanging in the house when I'm not home and you must be home by 10:00. "Well Dad I think you should at least allow me to get phone calls up to 11:00 on the days he drops me off just so I know he made it home." Maxine suggested. "Fine, that is acceptable." David said.

Maxine and Bryan were like Siamese twins joined at the hip. Where you saw her, he wasn't too far. If she was practicing at squad he was waiting for her in the car. School was out and they spent even more time together. She would spend time at his house and he would drop her off home before he went to the gym or to play ball. By the end of August Maxine was falling deeply in love with Bryan. If he told her to come by she would drop everything. If he told her to stay out a little later she would have Stacey or Liz cover for her. There was nothing she wouldn't do for him.

Now Liz and Stacey were feeling a little jealous. Bryan sneaked right in and took their girl from them. The whole entire summer they may have saw her about five times. Maxine and Bryan spent their summer together. School was back in and Maxine was now a senior. Maxine and Bryan kissed and fondled but that was about it. Bryan was ready to have sex with Maxine. Bryan's mom was going away for Veteran's Day weekend and he thought this would be the perfect time. Maxine told her dad that she would be at Liz's house for the night.

When Maxine got to the house Bryan was wearing a pair of basketball shorts with no shirt. He had the lights dim and had TLC's Red Light Special playing on the stereo. Bryan led her to the couch and sat her down. He kissed her on her lips and told her he loved her. He slowly undresses her revealing her pink matching bra & panties from Victoria Secret. He gently laid her on the couch. "Are you scared?" Bryan asked "I won't hurt you." he said. He began sliding her panties off of her. He began licking and sucking on her nipples in a circular motion. Between her legs was like a volcano waiting to erupt, he led his hands to her throbbing wet spot and began stroking it. She let out a moan.

It was obvious she was enjoying every minute of it. Bryan enjoyed the way Maxine's body felt against his, his shaft harden and before she could think about anything else it happen. Bryan was pushing his erect penis into Maxine, she let out a slight scream and he began moving up and down, she began working her hips meeting each of his pumps. Max had given up her virginity. He kissed her on her cheek and held her for the rest of the night.

Two days later Maxine told Liz and Stacey about her night. Stacey asked her those questions that every girl asks her friend when she has had sex for the first time, "Did it hurt? Did you bleed a lot? How did it feel?" "It hurt in the beginning but he was so gentle with me. He touched me in all the right spots. Once I got into it, he had my whole body trembling. It's like we are really made for each other." Maxine said in one breath. "Well I sure hope you guys used a condom." Liz stood waiting for Max to answer her question. "Well? "

"No, we didn't use a condom." Don't be stupid Max make sure you use a condom next time." interrupted Stacey.

"We barely spend time together. It's all about Bryan now. All I know is my birthday is next week and I know we are going out." said Liz. "You didn't even congratulate me on getting my license" yelled Stacey. The girls began screaming. "Oh my GOD Stacey you got your license!" Maxine was excited for her friend. "Yup and my sister is letting us hold her truck for my birthday...Maxine, you quit the squad. What's that all about?"

Bryan pulled up in his silver Honda Accord and honked the horn. "What's up girls?" The girls walked Maxine to the car. "Hi Bryan" Both girls said. They said their good-byes and Bryan and Maxine pulled off. Liz and Stacey liked Bryan and thought he was a really cool guy but they didn't like that he had all of Max's attention. He always seems to come just when they were together, like if he was watching her. Liz thought "After my birthday I'll say something to her I just want to hang out with my girl. "Liz you see Max didn't answer you about the squad. I wonder what's up with that." Stacey said.

The day after Bryan and Max had sex, Bryan told Maxine he didn't want her to be apart of the squad anymore cause he noticed how the guys were hawking her. He couldn't be at every game to make sure they wouldn't step to her. "Bryan I don't want to quit I've been doing this since 7th grade. I'm in my senior year why would I quit now?" "Cause I said so. What you like those niggas up in your face? You know all they want to do is fuck you." said Bryan. "Please Bryan, I'm not quitting." As she turns her back to walk away Bryan grabbed her by her hair. He pulled her down to the floor.

"I see the way you play around with those guys on the basketball team." "Bryan are you fucking crazy, let go of my hair." yelled Maxine. He loosen the grip on her hair and she jumped up and swung but she missed and he pushed her back down on the ground. "You are quitting the team or it's over." Maxine couldn't believe that he pulled her hair and pushed her." "You know what Bryan then its over." Maxine began walking out the door. "Come back here Maxine. I'm sorry I don't know what got into me." He followed her out the door. Maxine didn't really want to leave she loved him to much to go. "Bryan what's wrong with you. I'm in love with you and no one else." "So prove it to me, quit the squad." Bryan got what he wanted Maxine quit the squad the next day.

Max and Bryan had just finished having sex at his house when he asked her. "Are you cheating on me? I can tell if someone's been tapping my pussy." "Bryan don't be stupid. You are the only one I'm fucking with. Why would you ask me something like that?" It was Friday, the day before Liz's birthday. Maxine didn't want to get in a fight with him so she got up out of the bed and started dressing.

"Where are you going Maxine? I'm talking to you." he said. "I need to go home and help my father out with something. I'll see you on Sunday." she said. "Why Sunday I'll see you tomorrow." "Bryan I told you already the girls and I are hanging out all day tomorrow." Bryan said "All day tomorrow, why?" Maxine shouted "Because it's what we do Bryan. We celebrate each other birthdays together. Not to mention I haven't been spending time with my girls." "Well tell them you can't make it that I made plans for us." "I'm going and that's that."

"You must have plans to see some guy. Your not going!" he said." Oh you want to bet." Before she could say another word Bryan's hand met her face. "What the fuck did I say?" He smacked her so hard when she opened her eyes she had to recollect her thoughts. The tears instantly filled up in her eyes. "How dare you?" she yelled. She raced at him to fight him back but he smacked her again. Now Maxine was frightened. Bryan was yelling "Don't you ever back talk me. Who the fuck do you think you are?" Maxine was crying. She began getting the rest of her things. His mother knocked on the door. "What are you two doing in there? Bryan you better keep your voice down in my house." Maxine was trembling she tried to yell out to his mother but it was like he knew it cause he gave her a 'I dare you Bitch' look.

She ran out his bedroom door past his mother. Bryan's mother gave him a look of disappointment as he ran behind her. "Look Maxine, I'm sorry I didn't mean to hit you but you pushed my buttons and got me so heated. I over reacted. It won't happen again." He said. "Bryan I don't know I need some time. He went to touch her and she jumped. "I'm not going to hurt you. Go out with your friends and have a good time." he said.

Maxine was confused what did she do to make him so angry with her. When Max got home her Dad and brother were in the living room watching TV. "Hey baby girl! How was practice?' her dad said. "Hi dad, practice was good. I'm tired so I'm going to bed. Good Night." "Good night baby girl." She didn't tell her father that she quit the squad. She hated lying to him but she would have to explain that Bryan wanted her to do it. She was so exhausted from crying. She got down on her knees and said a prayer. "Dear God, Bryan hit me today and I don't know why. He said that I got him mad. I don't like when he's mad because he turns into this different person. Please allow me to say the right things and do the right things by him. So that he won't have to hit me again. I love him so much. Amen."

Saturday morning the girls met up at Maxine's house. They had appointments to get their hair done. Stacey and Maxine were getting wash and sets with a doobie. Liz got Shirley temple curls. We were glad that Stacey decided not to wear that ponytail. Angela dropped her Explorer off at the beauty salon. When she pulled up we thought she was a hustler at first. The truck had dark tint windows with some hot rims and all you heard was the music pumping loudly. She must have gotten a pretty good car wash because it was shining.

The girls got back to the house. "Maxine, Bryan said give him a call. He called you about six times. Please give that punk a call" Mike said. "What's good Mike?" Liz said "You know today is my birthday."

"How are you Elizabeth? Happy Birthday. So how old are you now?" he said. Everyone laughed. Mike was the only one that called Liz by her full name. "I'm eighteen today so is that legal enough for twenty-one. When are you going to give me a play." she replied. "Stacey you look good, I didn't recognize you for a moment." He said. He had Stacey showing off her perfect white teeth. Mike messed with the two girls because he knew they liked him. "Mike leave my friends alone." his sister said. "You girls have a good time".

Maxine didn't speak to Bryan after what happened yesterday. It wasn't because she didn't want to, she just thought maybe they were underneath each other and just needed sometime so she decided she would call him when she got back.

The girls were going out to eat to Jimmy's on Fordham Road. right off the Major Degan Expressway. The girls got dressed and were looking good. Maxine had on a black v-neck cat suit that showed off every inch of her curves and exposed much of her cleavage. Liz wore a pair of black tight jeans and a sexy lacy top. Stacey was dressed in a mini skirt and a matching jacket.   They   began walking to the car when Bryan called Maxine's name. She walked over to him. "What's that you got on and why is your breast popping out of it." he said. "Look Bryan please don't start." she said. "Yeah ok whatever. Maxine, I've been calling you all day. I miss you. Are you still mad at me?" he said. "No I'm not mad at you. I was going to call you when I got home." she said. "Happy Birthday, Liz!" he shouted. "Thank you." she said.   "What time will you be home? Don't forget to call me." "I'll be in around 11 o'clock" she said. Bryan watched as the girls drove off. Bryan punched the air, he was furious that Maxine would wear something out like that. He walked to his car and decided to wait for her.

The girls parked the car. When they walked inside of Jimmy's all they could hear was this loud music playing. They were greeted by a doorman, there were pictures of A-list people hanging on the walls, and to the left were video games. In the back of the place was the club where you heard the music coming from and straight ahead was the restaurant where a different kind of music was playing.

The scenery wasn't all that grand from we sat when you looked out the blinds you saw a corner store and gas station. Stacey and Max ordered Chicken with Rice and Beans, Liz ordered Steak with Rice and Beans. After they finished eating they had the waitress bring out a slice of cake for Liz and they sung Happy Birthday.

They were eating their cake when two guys

approached them. One guy was very short and chubby he had on a pair of jeans and sweater but the other guy was handsome. He was Hispanic and dressed to kill he had on a silk shirt with a pair of black snake skin shoes. They talked with the girls for a moment and invite them into the party they were having there. The chubby guy whose name was Rob offered the girls a drink. "We aren't old enough to drink" said Stacey. The Hispanic guys said don't worry about it. I'm friends with the owner. They all ordered two rounds of Pina Coladas. The girls took their drinks and thanked the men. The Hispanic guy Raphael didn't leave without Liz taking his number. She told him she would be calling.

The girls had a good time. On the car ride home Stacey was a little tipsy from her drinks so Liz drove back. "Maxine I'm thinking about going away to college. The school is having a trip in two months where you go visit different colleges" said Liz. "I'm so glad you changed your mind about going away to college. That trip sounds like a plan to me. Let's do it!" Said Maxine. The girls dropped Maxine off. "We need to do this every weekend." Shouted Liz. "You know it. Love you guys." Max said.

As Max walked toward her building she didn't notice Bryan's car parked out front. Max opens the door to the entrance of her building when a figure wearing a black hoodie jumped out at her. It was Bryan. "Damn Bryan you scared me." Maxine its 1:00 in the morning you said you will be home around eleven o'clock." "Bryan what are you doing here?" "Your hair didn't look like that when you left what's wrong with it? You been drinking?" he asked her. "It's called dancing Bryan. I was dancing and yes I had a drink or two." Bryan pulled Max out of the building toward his car. "Where are we going Bryan?" she said. He shoved her in the car. "Bryan I'm too tired to do this now." Bryan got into the car and he turns around towards Maxine and started his accusations. "So Maxine how many niggas was up in your face? Where the fuck you get that outfit from? Showing my fucking body off. That shit is too tight." Maxine was too tired to argue and since she told her dad she may spend the night at Liz's house she went with Bryan.

He drove to his house and parked in front. She laid back in her seat and poked out her lips. "Now you went dancing I thought you were just going out to eat. What you fuckin someone else. Niggas touched on my ass tonight."he asked. By now Maxine was tired and just wanted to go to sleep so she said in a sassy tone "Bryan, I'm not your possession these are my breast, my ass and my pussy." Bryan gave her look that a father would give his child when they done something wrong.

He smacked her in the head and her face hit the passenger door. He started yelling "You belong to me." He began grabbing her breast and her pussy. "These are my breast, this is my ass, this is my pussy and if you ever give it away I will kill you." When he said that, goose bumps ran down Maxine's back. She reached for the door but he pushed her back on her seat and began tugging at her clothing trying to get them off of her. "What are you doing Bryan? Get off of me. She was trying to fight him back but she was too weak. She stared crying and it made Bryan angry.

"Look at you, Shut up!. You make me so mad." He shouted. Bryan got up off of Maxine and said "Let's go." At this point Max was submissive she didn't know what to expect and she was terrified of him. When they got upstairs Bryan's attitude was calm but he became very emotional. He began to cry "I love you so much. I didn't mean to talk to you that way or put my hands on you but it's your fault that you make me so angry." She thought maybe it is my fault. I know he loves me because if he didn't he wouldn't get so crazy. Bryan touched her face and noticed she had a bruise on the side of her face. "You can say you fell down the stairs." Max grabbed her face and went to the mirror. "Oh man Bryan how am I going to explain this to my dad. He's going to flip." Max spoke calmly as she didn't know if the rage would spark again. "I'm sorry baby. I promise I'll never hurt you again. I just want to make love to you." Bryan said. Bryan kissed Maxine on her bruise and began to make love to her. With each stroke Bryan gave Maxine shedded a tear. She wasn't sure if it was because it felt so good or she was glad that he wasn't hitting her.

At school Maxine told everyone that she fell down the steps running from the neighbor's dog in Bryan's building. When she told her father the story he analyzed the whole scenario again and again until she got upset and told him to just forget about it. The abuse went on in the relationship. He hit her at any given moment. If she looked at him cross eyed, if she said something he didn't like. If she didn't want to have sex and that was the worst beating cause after he would beat her he would take the sex. It was getting harder and harder to hide the marks but each and everytime someone asked her about it she would get defensive and tell a lie. She lied to her father and friends. She even gave up fighting back. She blamed herself and thought if she could only change him it would be like it was in the beginning. Maxine found herself in an abusive relationship and didn't know how she would get out.

One day Liz and Stacey came over to Maxine's house. Stacey said to her "Maxine we are worried about you. You don't seem the same. You don't talk about college anymore. What's up?" Liz interrupted "You didn't even pay for your trip to go on the college tours, did you notice I paid for you.

Look, we found out that Bryan has been hitting you?

Someone saw him punching on you and told us." Maxine was embarrassed. I mean we fight. We have disagreements, but it's nothing. Sometimes I just make him mad. The person who told you needs to mind their business." "Do you think this is love Maxine?" Stacey sadly said. "Look he loves me and I love him. It's really nothing." shouted Maxine. "Well when you want to talk about it you know where to find us." Liz was so angry and was tempted to tell her father and brother what they knew. "How stupid can she be. If that was me I would leave in a heart beat." Liz said to Stacey.

After the conversation Maxine had with the girls. She did a lot of thinking and she knew it was wrong, what she allowed Bryan to do. If he loved her he wouldn't hit her or make her do things she didn't want to do. She cared for Bryan but she didn't love him the same way. She realized that she was only with him cause she was scared of him. The next morning Maxine decided not to go to school. She wanted to think how she could end her relationship with Bryan. She called Bryan to tell him he didn't have to pick her up today because she wasn't feeling to well. Maxine knew that Bryan wouldn't be able to come to her house cause her father already made it clear he wasn't allowed in the house when he wasn't home. "Well do you want me to bring you something?" he asked. "No that's fine my father got me something last night. My Aunt V said she'll stop in to check on me." "OK then baby. I'll talk to you later. I love you." Bryan said

Maxine cried and cried until she couldn't cry anymore. She went downstairs to get some air. When she got outside Lance was walking by. "Hey Maxine, why have you been avoiding me? Did I do something to you?" said Lance. "Hi Lance, nah you haven't done nothing to me and I haven't been avoiding you." "Are you ok Maxine? Looks like you have been crying." he asked. "I'm ok just not feeling to well" she said. Lance grabbed Maxine hand. "Well I hope you feel better and stop being a stranger and call me." He said. Right at that moment Bryan walked up.

"Hey Maxine glad to see you feeling better." Maxine's heart started racing. She knew for sure this was going to get her an ass whipping. Lance could feel the tension between the two. "Is everything ok?" he asked. "Everything is fine homeboy you can go now." Bryan said. Maxine intervne, "It's ok Lance everything is fine. You can go!" "Alright Max talk to you later. Remember keep smiling."

Bryan was really boiling now. His girl is outside talking to some kid she use to date when she's supposed to be home sick. "Why was the ball player holding your hand?" Max was scared. She walked slowly in the building so that the people passing wouldn't hear his sudden outburst. They got upstairs to her apartment and that's when he struck her with his fist. "You lying Bitch." He yelled. Maxine instantly thought he was out of his mind to hit her in her father's house, who could come in at anytime. Maxine tried to get away.

Bryan grabbed her and threw her into the wall, she fell and he dragged her into her room, he began hitting and kicking her. He put his hands around her throat and began choking her. "I knew you were a fucking hoe. What, did he just leave here Maxine?" Maxine tried to pry his hand from around her neck. "Bryan please don't." she gasped. After he finished beating her she ran to the corner of her room. Bryan walked to her and lifted her up. She screamed out in pain. He really put a hurting on her. "Go get cleaned up before your father comes in here" he said. "Maxine went into the bathroom and knew that today was the last day he would hit her. She had to get him out of the house before her dad came home. "You have to go before my dad gets here." she said. "Maxine what are you going to say?" he asked. Don't worry. I'll think of something." "I'm so sorry." Maxine rolled her eyes behind his back. She was tired of it all.

Maxine got dress quickly. She didn't have any noticeably bruising on her face but underneath her clothing told a story. A story of a girl being physically abused by her boyfriend. She had to go somewhere because if she stood in the house her father would know that something was wrong. She decided to go over to Liz's house. "What's up homey didn't see you in school today." Liz said. Max walked slowly into Liz's room. "I think I'm coming down with the flu or something." "Girl you look horrible. Why aren't you in bed?" Maxine started crying "I know". Max are you ok?" Maxine rushed into Liz's bathroom. Liz called after her but she didn't answer. Liz was worried now. Why was Maxine crying? "Max are you ok?" Liz said as she was walked in the bathroom. She saw her friend standing in the bathroom trying to nurse a bruise on her shoulder. Maxine tried to cover it up but it was too late. "Max, my God what happened? Who did this to you?" Liz grabbed Maxine and hugged her. "He beats me Liz. He punches me, kicks me and slaps me around. He forces me to have sex when I don't want to. He's the reason why I quit the squad." Liz was in tears because she felt her friend's pain. "Why did you stay?" "He gets crazy, but then he tells me he's sorry and he'll never hurt me again and I believe him but then it gets worse."

"Maxine you need to leave him you can't be with a man that does this; he can't love you and cause you so much pain. You need to tell your father. You know him and Mike will bust his ass. I'm calling right now." Maxine knew Liz was right but right now she didn't want to be judged or add fuel to the fire. "No Liz please don't! I don't want my father and brother locked up because of this." Maxine was now unsure if leaving would be the right thing to do. "Liz he said he'd kill me." Liz knew that this was happening but to hear it and see the truth was heartbreaking.

"Max you need to go down to the cops and get an order of protection. Max you need to go to the hospital look at you." It was no getting out of this one. She was in a lot of pain. Liz took Maxine to the hospital. At the hospital they took Maxine right away. It seems that he had fractured her ribs and dislocated her shoulder. A social worker came into the room. "Hello Maxine, my name is Ms. Dixon I'm the social worker here at the hospital. I need to ask you a couple of questions. "Who did this to you?" she asked. Maxine was quiet for a minute but Liz held her hand and she answered "My boyfriend Bryan. We had an argument and he got upset." "Seems like he was very upset. Do you want to press charges?" "NO! I'm fine." Liz gave Maxine a hard stare. "Maxine you have to leave him." said Liz. "I am, I just don't want him arrested."

Maxine had to stay in the hospital for a day. So Liz had to call her father and brother and tell them what happened. When her father found out what had happened he was devastated. How could he not know this was happening to his little girl? By the time Stacey got to the hospital Mike was pacing up and down the hospital halls. To think, he allowed this guy into his home. He gave information to him about his sister. Mike walked into Maxine's room "He disrespected you like this. Bitch ass nigga. I'm going to fucking kill him." "Mike don't worry about it. It's over Mike" "Naw it's not going down like that. Mike left out the hospital with rage in his eyes'. Stacey followed behind him.

Mike and Stacey walked to the front of the hospital when they saw Bryan. Stacey thought "what is he doing here." Bryan had called Aunt V and because she didn't exactly know what happened she told him she was in the hospital. "Hey Mike how is…" Mike rushed Bryan with his fist punching him in the face. "You faggot you want to hit on someone. Try that shit with me." Mike didn't give Bryan a chance. "You put my sister in the hospital. I will kill you. Bryan was in shock. How could she tell them what he did. "It was an accident man" he tried to stop Mike but he kept on beating on him. If it wasn't for the security guards Bryan would have ended up in the same place Maxine was in.

Weeks had passed and Maxine had several messages from Bryan. "Please call me. Don't do this. We belong together. I'm sorry; I didn't mean to hurt you." Everything that he promised her when he first started hitting her. Maxine finally spoke with Bryan. He had called her while she was on the phone with Stacey. "Hello" she answered. "Maxine please don't hang up. Listen to me. I love you. Please forgive me." He begged. "Bryan it's over. You hit me for the last time. I'm sorry but I can't do this anymore". The phone went dead. Bryan was furious. How dare she hang up the phone. He kept calling. Maxine didn't answer the phone and after that day she decided to get an order of protection against him. He wasn't allowed to come near her school or home, or even call her. She received several hang up calls but it suddenly stopped. So she believed he finally got the message.

Max's life seemed to be getting back in order. She was graduating in a day and she got accepted to the University of North Carolina. Liz was on her way to UCLA and Stacey decided to stay close to her new boyfriend Mike at John Jay. The girls were in the gym trying on their graduation gowns when Lance walked in. "Maxine, I'll be meeting you on the Tar Heels courts." he said. She was so ecstatic that he got accepted to North Carolina. They were going to be together just like he said. "Lance I'm so happy for you." she threw her arms around Lance and he kissed her. "Whenever you ready girl, keep smiling" he said as he walked away. Maxine got more good news later that day, her guidance counselor told her she could get a partial cheerleading scholarship. Maxine was on cloud nine when she left school that day.

As the girls was walking to the train, Stacey noticed Bryan's car following them. "Hey, I don't want to alarm you but I think that's Bryan car" she said. "Listen just keep walking I have my order of protection. I can't let him scare me. He knows its over." said Maxine. Bryan parked the car at the train station and got out. Stacey was nervous. Come on Max let's go." "Maxine, can I talk to you for a minute." "Sorry Bryan but you can't. Just you being here is in violation of the order of protection." She said calmly. "Look I just wanted you to know that I'm sorry and that I never meant to hurt you." Liz stepped in the middle of Maxine and Bryan as he began to walk closer. "Liz its cool, I'm not going to hurt her." he said. "How many times have you told her that and you did." she said. Maxine and Bryan's eyes connect and just for that moment she remembered how she used to love him. "Look Bryan I have to go." she said. "Well before you leave can I give you a graduation present?" he asked. "No, but thanks anyway" she said.

Bryan tried to keep his composure but he began yelling. You think you are too good now. What now you got body guards protecting you? We belong together Maxine and I promise we will be together." The girls were thrown back by his sudden change in personality but not Maxine she was used to it but she was stronger now and she said. "Bryan you need help. I haven't done anything wrong but fall in love with you." she said. That sparked a fire in him that was waiting to explode. By now Stacey was on the pay phone with the cops. I'm calling the cops. Leave her alone." "It isn't over Maxine. I promise you that." he said as he got in his car. Bryan wanted Maxine to hurt the way he was hurting and he was going to see they be together.

Maxine and the girls waited for the cops and they took the information. "Don't worry Miss we will find him." said the cop. "Thank you" said Maxine. Maxine went home that night and she got down on her knees to say a prayer. "Dear God, thank you for giving me the strength to stand up to him. I ask that you rid him from my life. I know that you are a forgiving God so I ask that you help him so that he won't be able to hurt another girl."

It was graduation day, the girls all meet up at Max's house. They were so excited. They talked about how they were going to miss Kennedy and how the next fall was going to be hard to get through cause they wouldn't be together. "What are we going to do without each other?" asked Liz. "Yeah I know. I'm going to miss you guys so much." Max said. "Get the phone, Stacey" said Maxine. Stacey answered the phone but no one answered. "They hung up" she said. As the girls began to walk out the house the phone rang again. "Hello this is Maxine." "Maxine this is Bryan I just want to know if we can talk. He said "I know who this is.
You can't call here anymore. Please stop calling." Maxine hung up the phone. Bryan thought he would give her another chance to talk with him but when she rejected him he knew that it was because of her family and friends she turned against him. As Maxine and the girls began to walk out the house she turned back to kiss her father on the cheek. "See you at the ceremony. I love you" she said. "Love you too baby girl." he said.

The girls were so busy laughing and talking that they didn't notice Bryan's car parked across the street. As they approached Angela's truck and began to get inside Bryan appeared. Bryan looked like he had been drinking, his eyes were blood shot red and he looked like a madman. "Maxine I need to talk to you.Let me drive you to your graduation." he said The girls were caught off guard." Bryan you know you aren't supposed to be here." Stacey said. "Stacey this doesn't have nothing to do with you. Maxine I need you. Please forgive me" he said. As Maxine stepped in the car he grabbed at her. Stacey ran upstairs to get David and Mike. "Let her go Bryan! Let her go she doesn't want to be with you." shouted Liz. As Liz stepped around the car toward Bryan and Maxine, Bryan pulled out a gun and shot Liz. Liz dropped. Maxine ran towards Liz. "Liz! Liz!" shouted Maxine. Blood was all over her. Bryan pulled Maxine by her arm and threw her into the truck. As David and Mike ran out the building all they saw was the truck speeding off and Liz's body lying on the pavement.

"Bryan what have you done." Bryan began yelling and pointing the gun at Maxine. NO! Maxine what have you done. All I asked was to talk to you but your family and friends are coming between us." he said. I can't let anyone stand in our way.

"She's not dead, Liz isn't dead, I know she's ok." mumbled Maxine. Maxine didn't want to die by Bryan's hand so she opened up the car door and jumped out of it. Bryan stopped the car. Maxine began to run but Bryan was right on her trail. You can hear the sirens approaching but they weren't in time. Bryan yelled "Maxine if I can't have you, no one will." He shot at her twice striking her each time. She fell to the ground. Bryan walked up to her with the gun in his hand he knelt down beside her. "Maxine all I wanted to do was love you, all I wanted was for us to be together." Just as Bryan raised the gun the police surrounded him. Drop your weapon and put your hands up. "Drop your weapon. " An officer shouted. Bryan turned to face the cops with the gun still in his hand "Freeze." Bryan didn't adhere to what the officers wanted. They opened fire shooting him six times. Bryan was dead.

"Dear God, Why didn't I leave him when it first happened? Why did I love him? I knew better. Oh please GOD, Please God pull Liz and I through this."

"Maxine can you open your eyes. Maxine if you hear me open up your eyes." Maxine opened her eyes and seen only light. 'Could I be dead?' Maxine wondered. She was in the back of the ambulance. Her eyes were focusing on her father who was by her side. The ambulance attendant was working on her. She tried to speak but the ambulance attendant told her to save her strength. "You have been shot twice, in the shoulder and in your lower back."

"Where is Liz? Is she ok?" she asked. Please save your strength Maxine." he said.

Maxine remained in the hospital for a whole month. She was told of her friend's death and was unable to attend the funeral. On Maxine's first day out of the hospital she visited her friends grave. Liz was laid to rest on March 22,1995, her tombstone read: Our guardian angel, Elizabeth "Liz" Ramirez.

Maxine laid on top of the grave and cried "I'm so sorry Liz. The bullet should have been mine and not yours. She blamed herself for Liz's death. Stacey and her family spent a lot of time helping her to get through Liz's death. Maxine was still hurting but she began counseling. It was there her therapist suggest she go to a meeting.

Maxine went to this meeting and found out there were so many other girls out there going through the same thing. Some were able to get out on time and some weren't so lucky. She learned to forgive herself for what happened and realized it wasn't her fault.

Maxine and Lance moved to Chapel Hill in the fall. He was therapy for her as well. She was able to love again and not hurt. Max began volunteering at a crisis center for women who were and are in abusive relationships. Everyday she thinks about how things could have been different but all she can do is share her story and hope it gets through to someone else.

Every meeting starts off the same. "Hello my name is

CONCRETE JUNGLE

Maxine and I was a victim of an abusive relationship. I didn't believe this could happen to me but when you are in the middle of it, its hard to have perspective, little by little Bryan took control of my life, where I went, what I said, who I saw, what I wore, what I did. When I finally realized it wasn't a healthy relationship it was too late he had already become an obsessive lover. He shot me and killed my best friend. You may not think you are in an abusive relationship and if you are you may not be ready for help. But please don't wait until it's too late."

Kimberly Smith is a native from the Bronx, NY. She moved to Lincoln, Nebraska in 2003. Where she now attends the University Of Nebraska- Lincoln

UPTOWN
UPTOWN

| David Torres

As I looked out the window of Jimmy's Bronx Cafe and gazed over what would be my new empire, I couldn't help but think, "damn is this really what I want?" Here I am having dinner with two of the most powerful individuals of the Gulf Coast Cartel. Although I always played with the Big Boys I knew I had to prove that I can really roll with them. I had plans to flood Washington Heights like a "Nor'easter Storm".

My good friend Arsenio introduced me to Pablo. Arsenio was a Venezuelan friend of mine who used to go to the gas station I worked at as a kid. I always admired the fancy car's he drove the clothes he wore and the way he presented himself. I knew he was some big boss of something. I would always compliment him and ask him if he ever had work for me to let me know because when I grew up I wanted to be just as cool as him. Arsenio would always throw me a twenty dollar tip every time he would come sit and talk with me. He would tell me that hard work would get me places, he also used to tell me when it was time, he would think about getting me a job with him. The funny thing was I didn't know it would lead to this.

Arsenio and Pablo were the top leaders of the Gulf Coast Cartel who were responsible for more than ninety percent of the cocaine brought into the United States. Here I was, David Perez the one who would be flooding the streets of Washington Heights with the help of one of the most powerful cartels in the country. Arsenio was a tall thin handsome looking man, with a pencil thin mustache. He looked like one of the men you would see on one of the Spanish soap operas. Arsenio looked a lot younger than the fifty-five year-old man he said he was. With his high cheekbones and green eyes he looked like he pulled a lot of woman in his day. I was listening to Pablo as he spoke to me, "You speak very highly of your crew. I just hope they are capable of handling such a large quantity of work." Pablo was shorter than Arsenio. He was not a very handsome man. His face was withered with wrinkles and scars, like a soldier coming out of war. His hands looked as if they could cut through stones. Pablo, when he spoke to you, always gave total eye contact. We always had mutual respect for each other. I would not be here if I didn't have confidence in them. These guys are the major players in the Heights. Arsenio knows me. I only associate with key players in the game, and that is how I got to meet him.

As we were awaiting my boys Chi- Chi, Juan and Tito,

I was admiring the sun as it set upon the buildings. The sun was beating upon each building trying to escape the grasp of the night that was soon to come. The number one train roared through to Nagle Ave. station where you could hear the foot steps of all the people coming from work and rushing to get home before nightfall. Pablo spoke breaking me out of my trance. "Listen, I am giving you a chance to make a lot of money here but I can't have any problems. I know these Dominicans are well known here but I can't have any problems. This is a lot of responsibility that I am leaving in your hands. I can't have you people out there like cowboys and Indians thinking this is the Wild Wild West when it's only the upper Westside. If you have a plan it should be well thought out. I can't and I won't take any losses." Pablo was very stern.

He was serious and I knew by the look on his face he wasn't kidding. At that very moment Chi-Chi was walking in. He was decked out in a black Canali Suit with a matching silk Bernini shirt. The kid was styling. One thing about my crew is that we all knew how to dress and to impress. Chi-Chi was the oldest of the crew. You could not tell his age from his looks. Chi-Chi was of medium height with an athletic build. He always carried around a bossy image of himself. Sometimes he would be a little to cocky which would always lead to episodes.

As Chi- Chi approached Pablo and Arsenio stood up from their chairs to greet him. Chi-Chi extended his hand and greeted both Pablo and Arsenio with a firm handshake. "Saludos hermanos. David has spoken very highly of the both of you. I just hope he has spoken as highly of me to you". As he glared at me he said, "I understand that you have a product that you wish to distribute here in the Heights. I would just like to inform you that we are considered the cocaine capitol of New York City. We have all types of individuals coming here to cop from us. If not from me from my people or some of the other major players located here. If your product is what you say it is and the numbers are right we can definitely work. If the product is weak and the numbers suck, than let's not waste each other's time." Arsenio let out a laugh and stared at Pablo. "I got to give it to him he has balls. I tell you what you fucking platano, what we are offering is a lot better than the so-called coke you guys are selling up here. And as far as the numbers are concerned I am here to sell a product that will show you more money then you have seen in your whole fucking life. Now if you think you are dealing with some two bit fucking Columbian from Queens, than you guys are mistaken. So you don't try to flatter me with your street code of the fucking Heights. I am a Businessman, my product can sell anywhere".

While Arsenio was making his point, Juan and Tito were at the side listening to every word he had to say. Juan was the papi chulo of the crew. When it came to women Juan had it down to a science. He was definitely a hooker. If he could get an MVP Award for laying women, my man would be the batting champion Juan had the look of a model and was always working on his physique, which always attracted a lot of women. With his Colgate smile and debonair mannerism it was hard not to get along with him. He was dressed in his Tannery West leather outfit. While Tito chose to thug it out with a Sean Jean outfit with a pair of Timberlands. Tito was not one to style much. He was always on this thug trip, rocking jeans and Timberlands all the time. Tito always carried a chip on his shoulder, like he had a grudge against the world. With his Pillsbury Dough Boy physique he looked like a linebacker for the NY Giants. He was definitely an intimidating individual who didn't smile much but would give his right arm for you.

At that very moment I decided to put my two cents

in and introduce the rest of my crew. "Gentleman, this is Juan and Tito they will be in charge of the distribution. So gentleman since we are all here let's start. The three gents that you see in front of you have control of all of the major parts of the area you see out here. Chi- Chi controls all of the blocks starting from Isham St. to 191 St and Broadway. Juan has all of 190th St. and Broadway to 178th St while Tito has St. Nicholas all the way down to 155th St. we have everyone from the blacks of Harlem to the white boys from Nebraska coming to cop from us. I can tell you that we can get rid of a lot of bricks for you". Pablo, interrupted by saying, "I have 250 kilos of pure cocaine waiting to be sold on the streets. You guys promise me that you can do that with no problems I can guarantee another shipment in two months. Now let's stop the bullshit and let me see what you can do."

Tito wasn't impressed at all considering he was always the short tempered one of the crew. "Having that amount of weight is good, but what about the work?" I said "I'm glad you asked because since we are all here we can now leave and get to work. There is a lot of product to move and we are on a schedule". As we all walked out of Jimmy's Bronx Café to the black super stretch limo Pablo had parked out front. Then we all got into the limo and started bullshitting about the plans we had. As the driver pulled off I suggested that we go over the 207th St. Bridge, so I can show them where they would be distributing their goods.

As we drove downtown Pablo seemed impressed by all the traffic that was moving on our blocks. He knew he hit the jackpot. As we were driving through St. Nicholas and 191th St. Tito noticed that one of his corners was not secured. He then noticed one of his workers being dragged into an alley. It appeared that someone was making an attempt to rob him. "Stop the car. Stop the fucking car now." shouted Tito. We were all wondering what the hell was going on. As the car came to a stop Tito ran out of the limo like a race-horse out of the gate at the Aqueduct. He ran towards the alley that his worker was being dragged into as fast as he could. At that point Pablo, instructed his driver to follow him and take care of the problem. The driver darted out of the limo just as fast as Tito did and caught up to him in no time. He was running so fast we wondered was this mother fucker a track star or what.

Tito approached the guy who was dragging his employee to the alley. The guy turned around and was about to blow a cap from his 9 mm when out of no where a knife was thrown from the limo driver into his throat. Tito turned around drawing his weapon and saw that it was the same guy who was driving the limo and was amazed at how this short greasy haired mother fucker just threw a knife from that distance and hit its intended target with no problem whatsoever. I had grabbed the steering wheel of the limo and was heading towards the direction that Tito and the Limo driver were heading when I saw Tito, the limo driver and the worker coming towards us. "What the hell happened"? "Just get in the fuckin car and shut-up". The limo driver said very calmly. "We don't want to wait here to answer any questions. Do we"? Shit. I thought to myself, I knew we were going to run into problems but not this soon.

"Yo Dee, this is part of the game. Mother- fuckin stick-up kids wanna be players, they gotta pay. Your man here is some kinda Rambo throwing motherfuckin knives. Yo that nigga got skills", Tito said glancing at the driver as we sped off down St. Nicholas Ave heading towards our destination. "Did you get your knife back Pepe?" asked Pablo.
"No Pablo, I had gloves on so there is no need to worry."
" Good, then let's get back to business. Do you people have problems with the stick-up crews up here?"
" Yeah". We have a crew called the NBK Crew (Natural Born

Killers) who just feed off the careless niggas out here. I had a few problems with them as well as my compadres here." Answered Juan

They are a bunch of young punks who have their noses in everything. It's just that no one has caught up with them yet. The leader of the crew Cache, his brother was a big time baller out here. He got bagged a few years back for killing his second in command for stealing. Yeah, I heard that nigga tortured my man for two weeks before actually killing him. He was some sick bastard. After he got popped he didn't want no big niggas to try and move in on his turf cause he knew he would be getting out. There wasn't enough evidence to hold him on a murder rap so they got him on some bullshit weapons charge. Word is he should be out in another year or two.

Pablo stared at Tito and said, "You looked pretty pissed off Tito. Que Te pasa? I've been having big problems with these faggots for a while already. It's nothing I can't handle." "Well you see, I have to worry, because your problems become my problems and if we have problems there will be big problems." said Pablo

"Pablo don't worry, because all problems can be handled very easily." voiced Pepe. We all had a look like this mother-fucker is crazy. Pablo just stared out the window. Arsenio reassured him that we were here for him, "We are compadres and will always be compadres. Let's go in have a drink and celebrate."

With all the talking going on I didn't even notice that we reached our destination. We were in front of The Trump Plaza on 59th St. and Columbus Avenue. As the limo approached the front of the building the doorman quickly rushed over to us and opened the door for us.

I was impressed by the way everyone came to greet Pablo as if fuckin Marc Anthony had exited the limo. We were escorted to a private elevator to Pablo's suite. Yo now this was living. He had three of the top floors just for him and Arsenio. I figured give me a while and I will be just as big if not bigger than him. We made our way up to the penthouse suite of his hotel palace. Tito had this bewildered look upon his face like if something was troubling him.I asked, 'yo kid, wass up?' "Yo, that nigga your man just killed back there was Cache's nephew." "What?" I said trying not to get anyone's attention "Yeah man, he was Yolanda's son. He was down with the NBK's. He was trying to set his mark."

"Yo, you know Cache is going to be looking for who-ever did this."

"Yeah I know but the good thing is that no one saw us. At least I hope not." "But what happened to Lil Man that he was setting up to rob."

" Yo, I told him to drop off the product at the stash house and lay low for a few. I told him I would spot him the dollars that he would lose for those days he wasn't going to be working. The kid is a good earner and I know he's trying to get paid." I looked at Tito and told him "we will discuss this later." I did-n't want to fuck up the good connect we had.

As we made our way through the suite, Arsenio directed us towards the library. Damn, I thought to myself this place looks like the Museum of Natural History. Look at all this artwork covering the walls. It amazed me how the ugliest paintings were so attractive to some people. And the funni-est thing is that they spent a fortune on it. I looked at Juan and told him with all the money I make off of this I'm gonna retire and open up my own gallery. Juan busted out laugh-ing and said, "What are you gonna do, put the subway cars you use to write on in your gallery? You dumb spic, that was graffiti that you did back in the days it was not art." "Shit that was art kid. You know what it takes to put up a burner on a train."

"Enough of these ghetto stories", barked Pablo, as he tossed us each a gym bag. "Each of you gentleman have two kilos in each bag for starters. I want to see how you guys will make-out with that. I am going to set-up a stash house for you to go and re-up once you have gotten rid of the product at hand. I expect all the cash to be brought to Pepe. He will meet you all at a specific location to pick-up all the cash. As far as the police are concerned I have all of that under control. This does not mean that you guys have a free pass to sell drugs in the Heights. It just means we have connections on the inside. We don't need you to go out there and start doing shit out in the open either. If you do get popped you will be responsible for the Weight."

"What about the stick-up kids out there?" I asked. "You guys are key players in the Heights and I'm sure you have a reputation in the Streets, if you are such key figures as you say you are this shouldn't be a problem." "Yeah but key players or not these niggas don't give a shit. They robbed from a Columbian connection that Chico had. Them niggas robbed a fuckin eighteen wheeler with100 kilos in it." Tito explained.

"That sounds personal. I guarantee whoever robs from me or tries to stand up to me will face a severe penalty. You just do what you need to do and come to me with any problems you have. Oh, one more thing. You are not to have any little kids working your corners or delivering any product and no disrespect to any law enforcement. I know they can be the enemy but remember it's always good to have your friends close but your enemies even closer."

We all left with our packages in our possession. We were all going to be dropped off at the locations of our choice by Pepe, and begin our venture. We all sat silently in the limo as Pepe drove us. We all knew what we were in for, but little did Pablo and Arsenio know that a war was about to begin.

Our first shipment that was given to us on consignment was gone just as fast as it was given to us. All of these people were open. Everyone was coming to the Heights to cop from us. Niggas were setting up spots all over the Heights. Every corner that was unoccupied was now being taken over by the low level street dealer and we were the ones supplying them. As our pockets grew so did our respect and power. We were becoming well known throughout the city, from the streets of Harlem to the alleys of Chinatown niggas were feeling us. Pablo wasn't surprised that we could move his product. He just wanted to make sure he got his foot into one of the most promising neighborhoods in the city. He knew his product was slammin'. As long as he could put it out in the Heights it was gonna sell.

With Pablo and Arsenio backing us there was no stopping us now. I had decided to set-up shop in the Bronx. I went to my old block and started to talk to a bunch of hustlers I grew up with. My man Jay, a Puerto Rican kid that my mother used to take care of, blew up over night. He had the mighty Edenwald Projects on lock down. I'm talking major weight.

"What's up Jay?"

"Yo, wass up Papa. Longtime no see. You still out there doing that Wall Street thing?"

"Yeah, kinda. I sort of put it on the back burner for a while. Which is why I'm here."

"Talk to me Papa. You know I always got you. You got some problems? Anyone I need to knock off for you? You know, anything for a brother."

"Nah, kid. Nothing of the sort. I have a little proposition for you. I see you have come a long way from dealing weed in the Plaza. So I just thought you might be interested in some work."

"Yo, you know I already have a nine to five here and

if you are looking to sell me some stocks and bonds Michael Bilken that's ok. But I will let you wash my money for me like you do those Dominicans." "I'm not here to sell you no stocks but I have this", as I tossed him the gym bag. Jay opened the bag and looked at me with that happy go lucky smile on his face. Opening up one of the keys and taking a hit. He looked at me with a look on his face like a kid who was just given a tablespoon of Castor Oil.

"Shit! Where the fuck you get this shit from. This shit is like that old type of shit we used to get. You don't find this shit anymore."

"I know. That's why I came to you. If anyone can get rid of it, it would be you." "So what do you say?"

"Well you know, I gotta check the numbers."

"Now would I try and jerk an old friend?"

Jay let out a laugh and said, "you better not because you know I can still kick your ass." "Well be careful I just might get my Mom to beat yours."

"You see, why you gotta bring Ma in this? You know she saw me the other day with some people and she gonna start yelling at me like if I was still a little kid. I was scared shitless though." She was like, "Joseph, you better not be doing nothing bad out here because you know if I hear anything funny going on I will whip your little white ass."

"Now how she gonna embarrass me in front of my peeps and call me by my government name. That fucked my whole shit up." I couldn't stop laughing cause Jay had that Chris Rock way of telling a story. After laughing my ass off I told him I had five kilos in there and I would be back in a week for the payout. He looked at me and asked, "nigga give me a number".

I looked at him with a face like a priest getting ready to take penance. "Son, for you fifteen a key." "Hold up Dee. First of all who the fuck did you kill for this." "No one my brother. You heard of all the shit that's flooding the streets of Washington Heights. Well that's me. I got a connection. I started out with money laundering while I was down on Wall Street and they liked my style and decided to hit me off with some work."

"So you that nigga they call "El Patron". Someone was telling me there is some cat in the Heights who put some work out there that got niggas flippin. I heard your product has even made it out to Boise, Idaho kid. You out there doing shit for the community, cleaning up parks throwing block parties for the community, sponsoring teams for the kids. Hell even donating to the PBA. What are you some kinda Robin Hood"

"Shit I gotta do something to keep the blocks intact."

Jay got up from his chair and gave me such a hug that he knocked the entire windout of me. "Yo, if you ever have any problems with those cats you let me know. I am here for you kid. And as far as the money (Jay then took out a briefcase from under the desk where he was sitting and counted all the money), "Here's payment for the kilos".
"Yo, come back next week with 15 more, these shits will be gone by then."
"You got it."

As I left Jay's place and got into my car. I started thinking. Damn, that's what they calling me "El Patron." I guess I could make something of this after all.

SAGA CONTINUES

David Torres is a native of The Bronx. David has since relocated to Westchester County and still to this day keeps to his grass roots. He is currently hard at work on his first novel "The Taking Of The Heights"

Shortcut Through Hell

| J. Lynn

There I was, all by myself walking through Hell. The sky looked as if it had been colored with black charcoal mixed in with blotches of gray and white. Small slithers of fog crept in front of me as though warning me to turn back and go home. So dark and chilling to my bones was the ambiance.

Broken glass bottles lay on either side as I walked with a heavy foot and my heart pounding louder than any college football band's drums. Garbage, pipes and shit adorned the path in which I walked. An array of tiny colored capped crack bottles lay empty all around me. Windows were chained and boarded up as it looked as if I was walking through a ghost town. I wondered when some tumbleweed would cross my path, but that was the least of my worries.

Graffiti was part of the concrete decor depicting, "R.I.P. CHICO" and the filthy language adorning the walls was something my virgin eyes shouldn't have witnessed. The sight, alone, of the writings and violent pictures of guns, skeleton heads, knives and drugs had me wondering about the artists of these deathly paintings.

The wind sounded like one thousand screams in the night the screams of those who were victims to robbery, rape, sodomy and a hard knocked life. Yet, I walked through this catacomb like gateway to destruction and despair. And why? Just to prove that I feared nothing and no one. Who was I fooling? What was I trying to accomplish by setting myself up to become another statistic in the paper headlines reading, "GIRL SLAIN WALKING THROUGH HELL: The story on page 3."

The truth is... fear gripped my heart until I could hardly breathe. The continuous beats of my heart were so loud that I would not have heard if anyone tried to come up behind me. Drops of perspiration turned into buckets of sweat as if though the sun, itself, broke through the cold winter night and wrapped its rays around me.

Adding a hip hop bop to my step and distorting my face as though I was The Game, was my own way of masking the intense fear and overwhelming anxiousness which lurked inside and about me. Except for the rumors and ill stories I had heard in school and from my older brother, I knew nothing of this place. The feeling of displacement rolled around me as I trespassed into this highly forbidden territory.

Others had always talked about Hell not scaring them and that they would walk through at any time; many stories revolved around scenarios of what people would do if anyone tried to mess with them had they actually walked through this undesirable place. Rarely was there a story that actually told of someone's true experience of physically taking a journey. Just a lot of talk without the actions of these fantasized tales.

"Pssst pssst...," someone called out from under a cardboard box. *Oh shit,* I thought. I skipped my pace but not too much to the point where I would have been looked upon for being frightened. And then, "Lightskin...come here. Why you walkin' so fast?" *"I'm not walking fast. I'm not scared. Why don't you just step off and let me mind my business and you do the same? Let me get to where I gotta go,"* is what I wanted so desperately to say, but instead I kept it moving toward my destination, praying the voice would not unveil its form to me. Destination? Would I ever get there? Damn, only the end to this gut wrenching excursion would tell that story.

The teddy bear softness of my bed and safe enclosure of my apartment is all I longed for. In fact, I should have been there. I should have been lying on my bed staring at the ceiling wondering what it would have been like to take this walk. But instead, there I was experiencing what I should have been imagining and more than anything; I wanted to not find out what this experience was going to lead to.

I fastened the snaps of my black and cream colored suede Baby Phat jacket and pulled my black cashmere scarf up around my mouth to block out the stench of sex, lies and murder. The fact that it was 44 degrees outside never crossed my mind, especially since I was burning with the desire for this little trip through Hell to be over.

On her knees with dark hair scattered upon the top of her head and a tan slightly soiled trench coat with low top gray Air Force Ones and blue dungaree jeans on, she gagged and withdrew her wet mouth from his member. "What the fuck you think you doing bitch? You ain't done!" He said this as he grabbed her head and forced himself back into her mouth. As he viciously jerked his pelvis back and forth, he then let out a loud obnoxious moan. "Yeah ho, that's what I'm talkin bout. Get the fuck off me!" he yelled at her as she fell to the ground. He than pulled the zipper up on his army fatigue designed pants.

Reaching into the inside pocket of his oversized red bubble jacket, he tossed a tiny package onto the ground at her knees. As she scrambled for the paper wrapped object, he stepped to her and violently took her chin into his hands, "Next time, have my money you filthy cunt! No more of these head games cause your shit ain't that tight. Move the fuck out my way!" And with that, he stepped away from this miserable mess.

Looking up for a quick moment, I could see the dried mascara stained face of a woman who obviously lost all hope. I squinted my eyes and zoomed in on this stranger. Wait a minute, this woman was no stranger. I knew her...but how did *she* end up like this?

Sheila Wright raised in Harlem by a single mother who gave her absolute all to make sure her daughter had the best of everything. And she did. Graduated at the top of her senior high school class and accepted into Clark Atlanta on a partial academic scholarship, Sheila had truly beat the odds of ending up like most of her friends who had dropped out of school and got on dope or landed themselves in jail or in someone's cold grave.

With a double degree in Business and Accounting, she landed a job at a top firm in Corporate America and broke through glass ceilings, concrete walls and metal doors which led her straight to the top of her company. A great feat for a black woman.

Enter Randolph Wellington III, a member on the executive board of Sheila's company - cocky white man that had everything from the time he was born, handed to him on an iced out platinum platter. Wellington meets Wright and they become close associates. "This will make you feel more relaxed. How do you think we all get through our days here at Vanson & Lang? Try it. Don't be afraid. You wanna stay on top of your game, don't you Sheila?"

Long nights of work in the office turned into even longer nights of coke bingeing by Sheila and her new "friends" at the office. But pretty soon, she lost all control and began a habit that led to her losing her job, her Madison Avenue condominium and everything she ever worked for. Stealing and sexing for money to get her next hit, she became entangled in a downward spiral into nothingness. Alienated from all who knew her well, this had become her life.

Turning my head with a quickness that surely would pain my neck the next morning, I tried to pretend as if I had not just seen what went on and what else could have gone down due to me staring in disbelief at what this animal was having this woman do. I couldn't believe it. How does someone with so much.... someone on top of the world... just let it all go down like this? I froze as he looked my way only for a moment before disappearing into the night. Breathing resumed. *Whew.*

She took the bag up into her bosom and tried to gather herself together. Oblivious to my pungent stare, she simply licked her lips, took her hand and wiped around her mouth. All of a sudden, she turned up her face and started making these gagging noises. Anxiousness began to set within as I quickly scanned the area, but it left as soon as it came. The gagging suddenly stopped. She stood still for a few seconds picking at her tongue, probably trying to tackle those remaining pubic hairs lingering about, before finally stumbling on her way. I don't think she even noticed me standing there. Another one bites the dust, or should I say... snorts it.

Who and why would someone do such a thing to another human being? Or maybe she felt like this was the way? Like she had no other options, but it ain't have to go down like this. What was in that bag? Drugs maybe? Most likely. Sucking dick for some blow? Damn. Whatever the reason, I did not want the opportunity to guess at that particular moment.

Clutching my jacket tightly to my trembling body, I looked all around me and gulped a deep breath; the remote atmosphere was thicker than molasses. Blocking out the whispers echoing from the dark, I walked ahead, not knowing what lies ahead. I happened upon an unbelievable sight that is permanently etched in my cerebral. "The Children Are Our Future" was spray painted in yellow high on the side of a wall and right below, on the ground, lay this light skin boy with a belt tied around his arm and the head of an intravenous needle sticking out of it. Probably no older than eighteen, his face told of a different tale, a desperate tale. This dude was strung out on what it appeared to be – heroin! *Shit! People still using that stuff?*, is what I thought to myself.

Jamel Lewis *a ward of the state since he was six, he knew all too well the meaning of survival. His mother was a bonafide crackhead. She sold and tricked for money and drugs, hardly paying any real attention to her kids. The oldest of three children, Jamel hardly went to school and often scavenged garbage cans for food for him and his siblings.*

There were times when the young boy had to wake his mother up from out of her stupors because there was no more pampers in the house for his two-year-old sister. He was alone and scared. Pretty soon Child Services was called, but not before Jamel had to endure four years of endless physical and sexual abuse from his mother's many boyfriends, "Here mothafucka! What you afraid of? It tastes just like a lollipop. Open your fuckin mouth, you little bastard!"

Rape and constant abuse became the norm as little Jamel went from foster home to foster home. At age sixteen, he ran away from a home and discovered a friend by the name of Jack Daniels. This friend would act as a comforter and help to temporarily drown out his troubles. With no money and living on the streets, he began prostituting himself just to get food to eat. Recently, he got so sick that he had to go to the hospital where he found out he had full blown A.I.D.S. Never having the chance at life and never experiencing true love, he was left in this cold dark world, "Hell". He gave up.

I quietly inched my way to see if he was still breathing. I shied away for fear that he might lurch up and grab me... and then it happened. Major flashback which threw me into a mind boggling loop. Yo, this kid used to go to the same school as me. *Oh shit! What the fuck!?* He used to always stay to himself a lot, and then one day, he just stopped coming. I just thought he was mad shy or he just didn't like school. Who does?

Now look at him. What a shame because he used to be such a cutie. Damn. Family? Friends? What could have led him down this road to self- destruction? The vision of his dark heavy eyes and dirty clothes lingered on my mind as well as the fact that I could do nothing. I said nothing. Just hung my head in heavy sorrow, made the sign of the cross with my hand and continued on my personal journey.

She jumped right in front of me, wearing a tattered blue sweater, dusty orange pants and black wool scully pulled far down over her head. "You can help a sister out?" I almost peed in my pants. She scared the shit out of me. I didn't even see where she came from, so busy with the image of that boy on my mind and the tears beginning to swell in my eyes. "Nah...," I said as I walked around her. Yo, this bitch actually grabbed my arm. "You ain't got no money for me!?, she asked.

Before I knew it, my mouth got bigger than my 5'6' frame and I yelled back, "What the fuck did I just say? Don't be fuckin grabbin on me! Get out my face before you get cut!" What the hell did I do that dumb shit for? I ain't have nothing on me. Truth is, this chick could have straight got me, right there, making me a permanent resting place in Hell.

Whatever it was that rose up inside of me worked because she just stepped back with a look of astonishment and then fear and then hurt, all in a matter of nanoseconds. "I'm sorry. I didn't mean to bother you sister. I don't know what came over me. This ain't me. This just ain't me."

Lorraine Andrews - *a former hospital employee living a relatively comfortable life saw it all slip away when she received a pink slip four years ago. Never quite able to get back on her feet, Lorraine soon lost the lease to her two bedroom apartment in the Schomberg Towers. In the short years, she and her eight-year-old son have moved from shelter to shelter as space became available and have even done a seven month stint on the streets once.*

Originally from Kansas, she had no family in New York and the few friends she thought she had, turned a deaf ear once she got down on her luck. The guilt and pain of seeing her young son come home from school crying because of the taunts from the other kids because of their situation was almost too much for her to bare. "Baby it's gone be alright. Momma gone make it alright, God willing."

She's tried so desperately to lock down another job but only temporary work that didn't pay enough was all she could survive on. She had no choice but to do away with her pride and get on public assistance. And when that wasn't enough, she had to hope the hearts of total strangers would open enough to give her a few pennies or food for her and her baby. With all the programs out there, it just hasn't been enough. Lorraine had to adapt to a life she has never known in all her 33 years.

And just like that, I had probably crushed all hope that she might have had... maybe the anticipation of a hot meal... maybe she had kids she had to take care of... maybe she's been on the streets just looking for a break or some crazy sob story like that. But how was I to know she wasn't going to use the money for a bottle of Henny or drugs or some shit like that?

Scared shitless and more nervous than a brother in the back of a police car, I called out to her as she began to walk away. I don't know exactly what it was that made me do what I did next because I didn't know this woman from a can of paint and I sure as hell didn't know her situation. She could have been another Sheila for all I knew... or maybe not. "Wait! Here...," I reached deep into my back pants pocket and handed her all the money I had. Maybe it was the deepness of her eyes, the hollowness that lay within, as they pierced through my soul and into my heart.

She looked down into her hand and an immediate downpour of tears streamed down her cheeks. It was only twenty dollars but I guess to her, that was like gold or something. Probably because nobody had ever given her that much at one time before, if anything at all. "Thank you," she managed to say through tears. She motioned to hug me, but I unsteadily stepped back. She caught herself and then, without another word, disappeared into the night.

I don't know what it was, but for a moment which felt like an eternity, I just stood there and I stared until this stranger's figure became nothing more than a silhouette of the night air getting lost between the smoke and fog. A stiff, iced wind cut across my face knocking me back into this hellish reality and the grim truth that I wanted out. And fast. This couldn't be what life is all about for these people. It just couldn't.

This was not for me, not at all. I had to get the hell out, find my way quick before it was too late. God help me...please. I didn't want to get caught in the whirlwind of this despair, this hopelessness, this upsetting truth. Nausea came over me all at once and my breath seeped heavily out of my lungs with my heart beating dangerously against my chest cavity. I quickened my steps in search of the end to this live nightmare.

Oh my gosh... I made it. 126th and Lenox Avenue was in clear view. There I stood, dumbfounded, in the middle of the street. And then all of a sudden, the high pitched Puerto Rican voice of my homegirl, Tee Tee, called out at me, "What up Lala?" Still in a daze, she called out to me again, "Lala? Mama, you good?" My concentration penetrated for a moment, "Hey...what's up Tee Tee?"

Somewhat confused, she stared at me and asked, "Lala, where you coming from? I know you ain't just roll through hell just now." See, "Hell" is what most people in the neighborhood called this particular alley, because it was usually where all the dirt went... the drugs...the prostitution...the abandonment of dreams. All the crackheads and "good for nothings" labeled by themselves as well as society could usually be found there, in this neck of town. It was a shortcut from my house to C-Town, where my mother sometimes sent me to go buy groceries. I could have taken the long way, but I didn't. I had to see. I had to know. And now I did. Without ever looking directly at her, I answered, "Yeah... I did." Tee Tee grabbed my shoulders. "You crazy? Aye Dios Mio. You stupid Lala. One of them crackheads coulda robbed your ass." "Yo, I'll catch up with you later," I said as I left my friend talking to herself. Tee Tee was right. I was crazy. If my mother knew I had walked through that alley after telling me time and time again not to, she would have beat my ass for sure.

"LaTavia? That you baby? Did you get everything?" my mother's voice called out from inside of the kitchen as I walked through the brown metal door of my apartment. I guess I didn't hear her because before I knew it, she was standing in the doorway to my room. "Hellooo?," she asked in a singsong kind of way. "Where's my groceries LaTavia?" I stared blankly, "Huh? Oh. I dunno." My mother, annoyed, said to me, "LaTavia, what were you doing out there? Talking to your little friends? You didn't even go to the store for me? Never again. Give me my money...now!"

I searched my pockets and pulled out only lint and candy wrappers. "On top of not doing what I asked you to do, you lose my money? Real responsible Tavi. Hope you know that's coming out of your allowance." Pointing her finger at me, "Now you know why I don't let you go to the store or hang out that much. You want me to treat you like you're fifteen but you still act like your five." Disgusted and with her hands on both hips, she just turned and walked away, "I'll be back, I'll go to the store my damn self."

I closed the door behind my mother and sat at my window staring into the sky. I pulled my worn Cabbage Patch doll close to my heart and mentally embraced my life.

It was done. No more imagining. All the wondering had been made into a brutal and mind opening reality. "Hell" is a place I wouldn't recommend to anyone. My desire to overcome fear had been met and yet I still had the yearning to go back. To help. But I might be the one who would need the help. I was lucky this time All I could see was Sheila in the alley shamelessly giving head...that needle stuck in shorty's arm...the look on the lady's face as she left with the money I had given to her...the overwhelming feeling of pain and the smell of piss and sex mixed with death and damnation.

Yo it's not a game out there. Shit is realer than real out there. As I sit here in the comforts of my home with all my name brand clothes and shoes and all this nice shit that we have, not knowing what tomorrow holds clings to me like saran wrap. The pain stricken truth of my hood... your hood... all hoods is this... It's a fucking jungle out there

---

J.Lynn was born and raised in Harlem, NY. You can get at her at Innersoulpassion@aol.com.

IT'S WHERE YOU AT...

| ANTHONY WHYTE

They were best friends from birth; and through their early childhood education, they were always together. On the basketball court, Andre Wicca was unstoppable. He scored at will and took over a game like Jordan would back in the days. Attend any Junior High School game; and in the fourth quarter, you'll witness Andre take over. He would own it. Fans marveled at his skills and the way he showed no fear in being the one taking that final shot at the end of a game. They would come to call him the master. To his homies, he was the man, to girls he was a lover, their heartthrob, the man to replace the other man that brought them out to the game. This is what made Andre who he was. Rick was more like a brother and would try to follow in his footsteps. Rick was persistent with his game to out do Andre; he would never really measure up, Rick finally gave up. For Rick it was his final basketball game. It was over. He was more interested in slinging in the drug game than dribbling in basketball games.

"I just wanna be fuckin' rich man, I don't care about anything. They think I'm in heaven but I'm living in hell, man, they don't know. I gotta be gettin' paper and stop fuckin' with this hoop dreams bullshit" Rick said. He then walked out of the gym. It was the final game of the season. They had taken the opposition down to the wire. It ended right there with another loss. This wasn't a life-threatening situation, figured Andre.

When Rick lost interest, his life became worthless. He lived to sling rocks and did that on the daily basis. For the first few years Rick was successful, he met Shirley and immediately fell in love. He would yearn to see her on the daily and she in return, felt the same way about him. While Andre spent time on the basketball court developing his raw athletic talent of being a top college recruit. Rick put in his time on the grind. He fine-tuned his skills in search of graduating with high marks as a big time street hustler. Occasionally they'd meet on the neighborhood basketball courts. The old friends would shoot hoops, challenge each other and generally horse around.

"Yeah and what? I can still run circles around you kid." Andre teased. "You're never gonna be able to guard me, son." Andre made a point of trashing his opponent's lack of defensive skills whenever he scored. It was obvious who the better player was. Rick made his points by trying to out-muscle Andre on the basketball court. This was impossible. Rick refused to give up on his quest and made every attempt to out jump, and rebound Andre. He wanted to do one thing better than his friend did and he never quit. However, that motivating factor kept Rick going. It was widely known that Andre had crept with Shirley and had been the reason for Shirley and Rick breaking up. She was pregnant with Andre's baby, so the rumor went. Andre was having the upper hand as they duel each other in a friendly one-on-one on the basketball court.

"What you gonna do? Try and wear me out? It's point game, Rick man. You trying to win a game against me is like Pac coming back alive. It's just not gonna happen, not in this lifetime, son. Maybe, if you're lucky and..."

"See that's what it is you're the one with all the luck. You're the one getting all the girls and..."

"I am the one. I mean you're simply not in my class kid..." Andre would say and as he packed away his gear to leave, Rick pulled out a gun and casually aimed it at Andre. "What are you trying to do man? Stop pointing that gun at me!" Andre yelled.

"Oh, see you the one shook now, boy?"

"Man, I ain't shook, but why you gonna be pointing a gun at me for? I ain't done shit to you."

"Yeah but that's why I can do it cuz you ain't shit."

"I ain't shit? I ain't shit? I'm supposed to be your friend, Rick. IT'S ALL GOOD TO FLASH YOUR GUN AT ME?"

Andre eyed his friend fearfully trying not to exacerbate the situation. Rick opened his mouth as if to answer but seemed to change his mind. He had the gun cocked and then he un-cocked it. Rick tucked the gun and walked away from Andre who was left shook, sweating bullets.

"Fuck you. You ball playin' ass, nigga." Rick shouted over his shoulders.

That proved to be the last time the two ever played together. They avoided each other. There would be basket ball tournaments where Andre excelled and became the toast of his community. Andre made a name for himself and was the hottest high school prospect on his way to Georgetown University.

Rick sank deeper and deeper in the mires of the drug Underworld. By the time he was nineteen, Rick already had two strikes against him. He was serving a four-year bid for the sales of narcotics. While in jail, Rick would brag;

"Yo that's my man," to anyone who listened. Everyone in the prison knew who Andre was during Rick's stay in prison. He always bragged about being the one who taught Andre a particular dribbling handle. "Yeah, I'm tellin' y'all, tha nigga straight bit that from me. That used to be my move." Rick said to other inmates.

"Yeah sure," another inmate replied. "That shit is fugazy..."

"I'll show an' prove next time you see me on the courts." Rick answered. Those who saw him play were convinced that Rick possessed some amount of skills, but nothing like what Andre displayed. In college, Andre never disappointed. He was an outstanding player. During a college basketball tournament known as March Madness, he was one of the premier players to watch. Pro-scouts wooed him and the NBA drooled after him. Through it all Andre stayed in college. Popular as he was, Andre had his share of love interests. He settled to a supportive cute sommelier called Tracy Watson. Her family was well off and she didn't care if Andre went to the NBA early or not. She was his number one fan. There were times when he wanted to leave on hardship for the NBA but his mother begged him to stay in school and get his degree.

"Dre you shouldn't worry about leaving school just yet." His mother suggested during the summer break before his senior year.

"But ma, the scouts are predicting I could go high in the first round." Andre countered.

"I know how important it is for you to live your dreams, but I want you to get your degree; it's important. After that honey, you will live your dreams. Just try to slow your roll. It'll happen in due time." Andre's mother said and gave him a kiss. The deal was sealed. Andre was a mama's boy. He trusted her decisions and she was not afraid to push her will on her only child. Try as he may and despite what all the scouts and agents reported, Andre did everything to stay in school. He committed to graduating. Eventually Andre did but not before his girlfriend, Tracy had given birth to his first child. A boy they called Andre Jr. The pressure was on for Andre to be the best teen father. He had to enter the NBA. He could easily declare hardship and enter the draft, it was an option that Andre considered but never made.

By then Rick was already back out on the street. He was motivated quickly and re-establish his business with new clientele. The illicit drug commerce began to pay off and the law anointed Rick the next drug kingpin status. He kept the neighborhood hopping and received props from all the users. Rick flaunted his new reputation around town. He wore jewels in abundance, like a rap star, his money made him a hit with all the chicks. It was then he met Monica, Tracy's younger sister who was enticed by the fast ways. She saw how the money turned over huge and she loved the way Rick treated her at first.

"I'm so happy I'm with a real baller. Those other dudes are so corny, working all their lives and have nothing to show for their labor." Monica said in a matter of fact tone. Rick stared at her for a second admiring her beautiful features.

"You're so beautiful I'm willing to put down the game just for you." Rick said and realized immediately that he did not mean anything he said. He laughed then they hugged and kissed.

Monica was only eighteen and was not ready for what was to come. She eventually became pregnant and all hell broke loose. Rick did not show her love anymore and would have his other girls at his apartment when she stopped by. She finally caught up to him, he was adamant about not wanting anything to do with her.

"I don't want you. Go home to your mother bitch. You can't stay here with me." He warned.

"What about the baby? I'm pregnant," she cried as he slammed the door. Monica saw the naked body of another woman in his bed when he answered the door. She was pregnant and had nowhere to go. Monica went and told her sister Tracy about the incident.

"He got me pregnant and now he doesn't even wanna talk to me."

"What did you expect from a drug dealer? Of course he's gonna kick your ass and call you names."

"But in the beginning he wasn't like that. He used to take me out and all that..."

"Yes back then everything was good, but it was not real. Drug dealers aren't real people. They're the type of people you create in your mind. He's a guy who has turned his life into a lie. I'll get Dre to talk to him. Maybe it'll be better if he spoke with him."

"No, don't tell Dre. I don't want him to know about my pregnancy and all..."

"If you don't get an abortion Monica, in a few months everyone is gonna know about your pregnancy."

"All right, you're right. Go ahead and let Dre talk to him." Monica agreed.

When Andre heard of the situation with Monica and Rick, he was very surprised and did not want to be involved.

"Your sister is gonna have to deal with this some other way. Rick doesn't care about no one but himself. He's certainly not gonna listen to me. He stopped doing that nearly six years ago."

"But if he knows she has other peoples who are willing to look-out for her maybe his approach would change." Tracy said.

"I don't know about all that. He wants to live his life a certain way and that's all to it. Why'd your sister get involved with Rick?"

"You gotta ask her that one yourself. But don't do it now, she's in a lot of pain, Dre. I guess all the flashy jewels and the big rolls of money was like an aphrodisiac."

"That's some bullshit, but I guess if I run into him I'll try if he'll listen." Andre said and ended the discussion. He was about to embark on the greatest journey of his life and did not want to mess with the affairs of Rick or no other. Because of his fiancée, he was willing to try to help.

The day would come when they both met at the Rucker Basketball Tournament. Andre was one of the prize team members of a team sponsored by the record producer, Eric Ascot. Andre was remarkable during the tournament. After the game was over, the two had a chance to exchanged pleasantries. A little chitchat occurred and Andre thought it was cool to broach the subject of Monica's pregnancy.

"So Dre, which pro team are you going to join, man?" Rick asked.

"It's up to the agent but it's probably gonna come down between the Bucks and the Cavaliers."

"Oh yeah? Sounds like you ready for all that."

"It's all up to the agent." Andre replied. He thought that everything was good between them. They were old friends and all the misunderstanding was settled. Andre did not feel any resentment or anger from his old friend. They seemed to have forgotten about the past. Both continued talking and Rick invited Andre to check his place out. Andre and Rick left the park together and headed for Rick's home in his new 645ci candy apple red BMW.

"You like the whip?" Rick asked as they sped through the streets on their way to his crib.

"Yeah man, this da shit. This is what I'm gonna buy when I get that contract." Andre said.

The car sped along until they reached the apartment located further uptown. They both exited and walked to the elevator. A few moments later, Rick opened the door to a fancy digs. Andre was pleasantly surprised.

"Welcome to my little jump-off."

"Dre, you gotta have a wicked jump shot to get you sump'n like this. Check out my big screen telly, nigga what!" Rick shouted boastfully.

"It's more like a movie theater." Andre rejoined. Rick walked around the apartment for a second proudly showing it's decoration. Andre lagged behind looking, checking out that while listening to Rick kick praises on his lifestyle. Rick's swagger was more intense as he had a chance to show off his crib. Andre was definitely impressed. He wandered and stared, his eyes wide as the lens of a camera. Andre eyed the place. "You're living large; you're doing good man, but yo, I'd like to know about Monica." Andre said. He glanced away from the lavish interior of Rick's apartment. Rick poured himself Moet without offering Andre another look. He sipped and Andre wondered if this meant anything. He pressed. "So Rick what's happening with that thing with Monica?" Rick finally glanced over and acknowledged the question.

"Monica? Who da fuck is Monica?" Rick asked. Andre stared in disbelief. He wasn't quite sure if Rick was for real or not. He wondered for a minute whether to drop it but he knew Tracey would ask questions. Andre knew he couldn't disappoint Tracy, she would never let him forget it. He might as well get another girlfriend. He didn't want to continue but felt he had to ask other questions. Rick sipped champagne and admired the watch on his wrist.

"I got beef with muthafuckin police; I got beef with outta town niggas tryin' to bag me for my muthafuckin money. Man I don't give a fuck about a muthafucking bitch. When D's come kick ma door down, ain't no woman gonna want me. Cuz I ain't got no cheddar for their ass. Look man fuck a bitch.

"I hear you but what if you could do sump'n for someone?"

"I'm only doing shit for delf. Dre check this out.

"What?"

"This fucking watch shining on my wrist, my man. I had all the diamonds put up in it." Rick said nodding approvingly. "These fools caught me for two-hundred and fifty g's." He spoke with verve but it sounded like empty boast to Andre. He sat there wearing a bored look until he yawned uncontrollably. While Rick crack another bottle of bubbly and poured himself another. He finally offered to pour a drink for Andre.

"Nah, man I'm good. It's time for me to head up outta here," Andre said and got up to leave. "I'm tired as hell, man. You know balling all day. I'm trying to go in the first round. I want to see as many teams as possible." Andre was just about to get up when the doorbell rang. Rick checked the security video and let the person in.

"Yeah man I hear you and wish you all the best. Even though me and you had our differences I still felt good when I hear the muthafuckin' announcer screaming your name". Rick said. Then he mimicked the announcer. "Andre Wicca steals the ball beats two defenders down court, spins and lays the ball in. I just be so proud, it used to bring tears to my eyes...I'm telling you I'd be sitting in my bin crying; when you took a loss it's like I lose too, Dre. That's how it was, we're like brothers from another mother." Rick said and extended his open palm. Andre seemed reluctant for a beat then slapped Rick's extended hand. "Ah...I thought you were gonna leave me hangin' homie." They shook hands and hugged.

"Yo, Rick man I gotta bounce up outta here" Andre started to say and the doorbell rang.

"Hold up a sec. Let me get this door." Rick said and casually walked to the door. Three scantily dressed girls walked in with shopping bags.

"Happy birthday, Rick!" They all chorused and smiled. They then began to sing. "Go, go, go shortie it's your birthday. We're gonna party like it's your birthday and we don't give a fuck if it's not your birthday..." The girls screamed and shouted. "Happy birthday Ricky baby." Rick smiled from ear to ear.

"It's your birthday?" Andre asked and wondered why he did not remember. Time had passed between them.

"You don't remember huh? Oh yes it is my birthday." Rick said. "Don't you remember? Either that or it's Christmas." He laughed and grabbed a handful of ass.

"Yo man I'll have a drink to your birthday." Andre said. The doorbell rang. This time Rick did not check the security camera. He busied himself feeling on tits and ass. He allowed one of his singing guests to get the door. Caution was thrown to the wind, while he had white stuff going up his nose. Rick never gave it a second thought. With all the enemies he had, the list was too long not to check the security camera.

"Get that, get that..." Rick shouted excitedly as doorbell rang. Andre watched a girl shoved spoons of cocaine up Rick's flared nostril until his eyes bugged. Andre's mind told him it was time to leave but when he saw the girls coming out of their already semi clad state, his body told him to stay. He was enjoying the party with the drug king pin who used to be a friend. Andre excused himself to the back to call his girlfriend letting her know things were not going as planned. He was not getting through to Rick and he was on his way home. Unknowingly then by this time the door had opened. There were no sudden outburst of gunfire but rather the caterers Rick had ordered. Behind them was Monica. She was coming to handle Rick herself. When she witnessed the cocaine sniffing birthday bash she snapped. Rick never imagined the same 22-caliber pistol he gave her is what would end his life. At this time Andre hears the shots. He sticks his head out and sees Monica blasting away he yells out " Monica" but she was in a zone. She didn't even realize it was Andre, as she turns and opens fire. Andre was killed. Nothing came of it except a small caption in the back of the Daily Newspaper declaring "NBA Prospect Gunned Down in a Drug Deal Gone Bad." It's the way it is in da Concrete Jungle!!.....

Anthony Whyte is the Essence Best selling Author of "Ghetto Girls." To his credit he also has written Ghetto Girls Too, Streets of New York, Vol.1. and is the CEO of Augustus Publishing, Inc.

WE AT JACKSON PRESS COROPORATION ARE HERE TO BRING TO YOU, THE READERS, CULTURAL LITERACY. AS PEOPLE FORGET THE AIR UNTIL IT IS THIN OR FOUL, PEOPLE, FORGET ABOUT CULTURAL LITERACY. THAT IS WHERE WE COME IN.

THIS COMPANY WAS FORMED BY THREE MEN WITH THE GOALS OF ESTABLISHING AUTHOR'S CAREERS AS WELL AS BRINGING YOU URBAN LITERATURE AND TALES THAT WILL MAKE YOU READ, THINK AND REACT. WE WILL BRING YOU THE MOST COMPELLING BOOKS YOU WOULD WANT TO ACQUIRE. NO STONE WILL BE UNTURNED, THE READER WILL NOT BE DENIED. WE WILL FACILITATE THE JOURNEY WITH EACH AUTHOR SO THAT OUR READERS WILL NOT FORGET; CULTURAL LITERACY IS IN THE AIR OF INTELLECTUAL INTERCOURSE!

"If your actions inspire others to dream more, learn more, do more and become more, you are a leader."

John Quincy Adams
(American 6th US president (1825-29),

Thank You

SHANNON HOLMES

EVERYTHING AIN'T FA EVERYBODY

COMING SOON SUMMER 2005

HIT THE STREETS AND COP THE HOTTEST URBAN FICTION BOOKS ON THE BLOCK

GHETTO GIRLS (SPECIAL EDITION)
ANTHONY WHYTE

GHETTO GIRLS TOO
ANTHONY WHYTE

GHETTO FALSEHOODS
ANTHONY WHYTE

STREETS OF NEW YORK VOL.1
ANTHONY WHYTE / MARK ANTHONY / ERICK S. GRAY

STREETS OF NEW YORK VOL.2
ANTHONY WHYTE / MARK ANTHONY / ERICK S. GRAY

STREETS OF NEW YORK VOL.3
ANTHONY WHYTE / MARK ANTHONY / ERICK S. GRAY

COMING SOON FROM AUGUSTUS PUBLISHING

GHETTO GIRLS 3 SOO HOOD
BY ANTHONY WHYTE

THIS BAG IS NOT A TOY
BY ANTHONY WHYTE

OFF DA HINGES
BY ANTHONY WHYTE

Augustus Publishing.com

NIKIA COMFORT

TAMING THE PHOENIX

COMING SOON ON
JACKSON PRESS

JACKSON
PRESS

ORDERFORM

NAME _____

COMPANY _____

ADDRESS _____

CITY _____ STATE _____ ZIP _____

PHONE _____ FAX _____

EMAIL _____

TITLES	PRICE	QTY	TOTAL
1. CONCRETE JUNGLE	14.95		

SUBTOTAL			
SHIPPING			
8.625% TAX			
TOTAL			

Inmates pay $10.00
(plus shiping)

JACKSON
P R E S S

SHIPPING CHARGES
GROUND ONE BOOK $4.95
EACH ADDITIONAL BOOK $1.00

Make all checks payable to:
Jackson Press Corp.
P.O. Box 690344 Bronx, New York 10469

JacksonPress.com
info@jacksonpress.com